THE OTHER GUY

By Cary Attwell

Text copyright © 2012 Cary Attwell
All Rights Reserved

This is a work of fiction. Names, characters, corporations, institutions, organizations, events or locales in this novel are either the product of the author's imagination or, if real, used fictitiously. Any resemblance to actual persons, living or dead, is entirely coincidental.

Chapter One

Stop me if you've heard this one. A plucky heroine sashays onto the silver screen, her slender arm linked to that of a bland chump. A diamond sparkles on her left hand. Their wedding plans come nicely along, he agreeably accommodating to her needs and whims, she acutely aware that this is a fault in his genetic make-up she must overlook.

Meanwhile, the actual love of her life, a man who, at some point prior, probably broke her heart, gets thrown into the mix and spends much of his allotted screen time being extremely handsome as well as something of a freewheeling bastard.

But then, on some pretext, Good-Looking Bastard realizes that the love of a good woman (i.e. Plucky Heroine) makes him want to change his ways, till death do him and Plucky Heroine part.

And we all root for them to realize they're meant for each other, mostly because they are exceptionally pretty together, and also because The Other Guy isn't on the movie poster, so you know he's doomed to be sidelined right around the eighty-two-minute mark.

That, and because being raised on a steady diet of meet-cutes, happily ever afters and butter-flavored popcorn instills in our hopeful hearts the illusion that sometimes good-looking bastards are actually Good-Looking Bastards with Secret Hearts of Gold.

(Where the popcorn comes into play is that the properties of its questionable flavoring in some of the microwaveable varieties may actually have a hand in causing dementia, but that's for another, more depressing story with a Good-Looking Bastard Neurologist in it.)

Eventually, after a series of misunderstandings and at least one ill-advised dance/karaoke/toilet scene, the movie culminates in Good-Looking Bastard racing to the church to stop the wedding. The Violin Strings of True Love soar, he commandeers a microphone to deliver a heartfelt speech, Plucky Heroine's eyes shine with tears, and away they whisk into the sunset, for what we can only assume will be a lifetime of quippy banter and incredibly hot sex.

The end.

Except not really. Not for The Other Guy, whose only sins so far have been toting around a basic sense of human decency that restrains him from barging into other people's nuptials to filch someone else's fiancée and lacking the manly wherewithal to grow designer stubble.

What do you do, then, when you're The Other Guy? When you're literally left at the altar, with a hundred of your friends and family, and hers, simply *gaping* at the former shell of yourself you're sure to become after a blow like that?

Run?

Well, I would've, but there was no way we were getting our deposits back on the reception site and all that fancy catering.

"Oh well," I said to the church at large. The echo of the doors banging shut in the wake of my ex-fiancée and her new dick of a boyfriend's exuberant exit was still reverberating off old stone and vaulted ceiling. "There's a free bar at the reception."

Which, of course, *I* was paying for, but that seemed a trivial consideration in comparison to the immediate prospect of sweet, shit-faced oblivion.

Pro tip: He will be righteously indignant on your behalf, but do not let your best man snarl at the less subtle of your guests to "Take a picture; it'll last longer," as this only encourages the world's most literal-minded wedding photographer to actually take a photo series of you falling apart inside.

(Pro tip footnote: Do not, out of charity, hire your fiancée's idiot second cousin to be your wedding photographer, no matter how many community college photography classes he says he's taken. There's a reason you never liked him, and this is exactly why.)

The funny thing is that this has happened before. Okay, not exactly *funny*, and not exactly on these terms -- I haven't, thankfully, been jilted at the altar twice (though, had this been the case, someone might find it entertaining enough to make a movie about me, and I would demand to be played by Jeremy Renner; yes, my arms look exactly like that, thank you for asking).

I have, however, been the guy, that guy, with whom women wet their feet when lifelong commitment becomes less of a faraway concept and more along the lines of *oh my god college was five years ago everyone on my Facebook news feed is manufacturing babies on a heavily expedited schedule I did not get that memo.*

And once they understand what a lifetime with a financially, mentally and emotionally stable person (i.e. me) looks like, that's when they decide their first college boyfriend was *the* boyfriend to end all boyfriends, and I was merely a stepping stone on their path to self-discovery.

Thank you, Emory, they say.

Go to hell, you poopface, I think.

Take care, I actually say, as a full-fledged member of the The Other Guy Club, which espouses doormat gallantry as its first basic tenet, even -- especially -- in the face of being dumped (*at the altar*) by a flighty young lady for some bestubbled adonis who probably wrecks impractical European sports cars as a side hobby.

I saw an oldish man once, outside a coffee shop, yelling about Jesus and things needing to be cleansed; he made a particular point to call every woman who passed by a Jezebel. At the time I was frankly relieved when the barista quietly dialed the neighborhood police, but I am beginning to see his point. Perhaps he has a newsletter I could subscribe to, maybe a distinguished publication like *Women Suck Weekly*.

Okay, fine, it's possible that I am being unfair to the approximately three and a half billion women in the world who haven't left me for her first college boyfriend, and just because something has happened twice doesn't conclusively make it a pattern. But twice! That's suspicious, at least.

Or maybe it's just me. It's probably me. Oh, Christ.

The party, loosely termed, ended before eight-thirty, which, even by my standards, was pretty pitiful. I suppose the free flow of cheap wine wasn't quite enough to liquor away the sight of the forsaken groom, sapped of all dignity and even his will to make a drunken wretch of himself in front of his nearest relations.

It wasn't that I didn't want to, it was just that I had much better vodka at home with which to besiege my liver more efficiently, and a comfy terrycloth robe that would absorb nicely the inevitable flood of snot and tears and, let's face it, probably throw-up. I had rented my tux after all; I didn't want it to get *gross*.

What should have been the receiving line turned into some parody of a funereal march, and I slumped at the door, shaking hands and taking solemn claps on the shoulder.

Mom gave me a tight hug, and Dad squeezed the space between my shoulder and clavicle a little harder than usual, but that was about all I got out of them. We're stoic, Midwestern types; emotional displays are foreign and faddish to us.

Even our priest, a man who had poured the holy water at my baptism and watched me grow from Sunday to Sunday until I lapsed out of churchgoing, could offer no better comfort than the fact that God occasionally enjoyed fussing around with doors and windows. I wanted to discuss whether God had considered the possibility of installing cat flaps in my life, but the rest of the line, eager to hasten their respective escapes from my blank desolation, jostled Father Stanley away and into the night before I could ask.

Everyone else did their best to tilt their heads at me that auntie-patented, *oh, you poor thing* sort of way, and the less generous of my kinfolk stole away with the gifts they'd dropped off earlier, when I had still been on track to live the kind of life that included a heart-shaped waffle iron.

When it was just me and my best man left, Hal thumped at my back with a giant, flat palm, temporarily rearranging the alignment of my spine to indicate his succor. Manly, you know. He was, at least; I just stumbled forward at the blow and coughed a bit.

He helped me cart the remainder of the gifts home, stockpiling them in the living room, careful to keep their cards attached so I could return them to their senders later on, because what was I going to do with four sets of embroidered sage green towels anyway, besides enjoy the luxury of crying into a different one every day?

"Michelle wasn't right for you," he said over crossed arms, after sticking around to make sure I didn't drown myself in the shower.

I sank onto the sofa, an old three-seater upholstered in dark blue tweed. Were I a poetic sort I might be tempted to compare the state of my withered soul to its melancholic hue. *Roses are red, this couch is blue, my fiancée left me, and I hope she gets the bubonic plague.* I'll take my Walt Whitman Award in the form of cash and a decade's worth of psychotherapy, please.

"That's what you said about Dani, too," I pointed out, feeling sad and small, swallowed by my bathrobe, water trickling down the soggy curls at the back of my neck. In the empty screen of the wall-mounted television directly opposite, over an equally vacant fireplace, I could make out the reflection of a person destined for a lifetime of microwaveable meals and a disturbing number of cats.

Hal scrubbed thoughtfully at his beard, a thick, dark blond mass of bristles of which I had always been secretly jealous, never having been able to get much out of my own face than thin, irregular patches. He shrugged. "Yeah, well."

It could've meant *Yeah, well, and I was right*, or maybe *Yeah, well, you could obviously do better*, or something else entirely, but I didn't have the energy to pick his taciturn, lumberjacky mutterings apart.

"I think," I said, creating an instant damp spot on the back of my couch as I dropped my head to face the ceiling, "I'm defective."

Hal narrowed his eyes minutely. "Don't be stupid."

"Okay," I agreed.

"What are you going to do now?" he asked.

I lifted my head and looked around the room, hoping to glean some inspiration from my stolid furnishings, which proved useless. Michelle's ghost lingered everywhere, her fingerprints on every nook and cranny of my life for the past three years we had been together. I doubted they would erase themselves, even if I asked nicely.

We had spent all this time building and building to a single moment, a crux of a moment; there had even been a rehearsal specially arranged for it. When things come with rehearsals, you tend to let your guard down about everyone else going off-script, and then when it happens, you're left standing and staring like the world's greatest idiot while they simply move around you.

The pile of wedding gifts in the center of the carpet glittered at me, mockery evident in their department store wrappings for my failings, judgment in their gauzy bows and fripperies. Peeved, I pushed myself off the sofa, headed for the bedroom.

"I'm going to pack," I announced.

"And...?" Hal prompted, following my strides with no small measure of dubiousness at my sudden proclamation.

"And," I said brightly, yanking a suitcase from the closet, "I'm going on my honeymoon. By myself. Michelle took off to god-knows-where with James Dean's robot clone, and I have the tickets still for Thailand. I'm going on vacation."

"Oh... kay..." said Hal, and I could tell that he was trying to gauge just how crazy my eyes looked. Probably somewhere around a seven.

"Look," I said, aiming for reasonable, as I sniffed a couple of T-shirts and mashed them into the suitcase, "it's too late to cancel all the reservations and recoup all those costs. There's the plane tickets, the resort... I think-- I think we reserved a couples massage at the spa..."

I paused in my indiscriminate packing for a moment, wondering where to find a confirmation of the spa thing. Maybe they would let me split it into two separate sessions and I could get both massages. I'd be the pliantest boy on the block. Things were looking up already.

Hal frowned. "Are you sure this is a good idea?"

"Uh, live in a tropical paradise for a week and sip fruity drinks with umbrellas in them by the pool? Yeah, Hal," I said, cranking up the sarcasm far past eleven, "that's a fate worse than death. I don't know what I was thinking."

"No," he said, stretching the word out longer than was healthy for it, "I was thinking more like going on a honeymoon without a wife."

I dropped a sock and looked up at him, stung. "Don't rub it in, man."

He raised his palms in surrender. "Sorry. Just saying."

"Yeah," I sighed. "I know."

I'll grant that the whole idea was potential grounds for institutionalization, or at least careful psychiatric observation, but I needed to do something, anything to get away from all of this. I was helpless, I was the one left behind, I was the one who wasn't good enough.

I think it's safe to say that when I was a kid dreaming of the endless possibilities of what my life could become when I grew up, none of those things came close to cracking the top ten. And even when I was a teenager, a college graduate, a master's candidate, with hopes of professional superheroing long since dashed, it never crossed my mind that I would end up an actual failure of life.

And if that didn't qualify me enough to get the hell out of the apartment, the city, the continent infested with mementos of the girl who'd made me a failure, then I didn't know what would.

Plus, I had taken a whole week of leave from work, and I really didn't want to go in on Monday having explanations expertly spun on the tip of my tongue, only to have Marybeth at reception go all *Oh, honey* at me as soon as I walked in.

At least in Thailand, people wouldn't look at me as though I'd been repeatedly kicked in the gut and ply me with trite platitudes. They would ply me instead with fresh coconut juice and elephants and fried food on a stick for being an intrepid traveler and valued contributor to the local tourism industry. There, I would be *useful*.

Or at least as useful as a pasty white person wandering around confusedly in ill-fitting bermuda shorts and demanding a one-person couples massage from time to time.

And at least I'd be good at it for a while.

***

There are times when you're so lost that even reaching for the bottle of vodka above your fridge seems too monumental an effort to undertake, let alone imbibe its contents, and that was probably the reason I managed to finish packing, order a cab and make it to the airport on time the following morning.

It was a smallish victory, but I doggedly chose to be proud of myself for being able to function.

Nobody at security thought I was particularly of interest, and if anyone suspected I was secretly dying inside they certainly didn't mention it. Not high priorities on the security threat scale, we of the shriveled souls, capable of not much more than curling up in the fetal position and moaning every now and then.

I slogged over to my gate with plenty of time before boarding but was spared the half hour's worth of aimless wandering up and down the terminal when my cell phone rang.

It was an international area code. Hal must have told her.

I put the phone to my ear.

"Oh my god, Em," a voice shrilled the second the connection clicked open. "I can't even believe that bitch. Are you okay? Do I have to come home and kick her ass? Because I will, if you want me to. No questions asked."

"Hello," I said, smiling in spite of myself. "Who is this?"

"She's an asshole," Linn carried on. "She doesn't deserve to lick the bottom of those boots you wore when you went to work at your uncle's dairy farm that one summer and had to trudge around in cow shit all day."

My brow furrowed, and I glanced around askance. "I don't even remember telling you that. Anyway, didn't you know you're not supposed to insult my ex right after? I mean, what if we got back together?"

"What? Screw that. I always thought you deserved better than her."

"Yes," I said. "I know."

I did know. Linnea was honest to a fault, and I loved that about her, even if I didn't want to sometimes. She had a low tolerance for bullshit and therefore never considered indulging in it herself. We'd sat next to each other at our graduate school orientation and had been friends ever since.

Naturally, she'd been invited to the wedding but, now practicing in Edinburgh and heavily pregnant with her second child, mere weeks away from popping, hadn't been able to come. Which I think was for the best, as Michelle would now be missing several teeth and probably a clump of hair if she had pulled her runaway bride routine with Linn in attendance. Good old Linn.

"And I swear to god, Em," she plowed on, "if you even think about taking her back after what she did to you, I *will* book the next available flight back so I can slap you in the face."

Less good.

"Isn't having kids supposed to make you a happier person?" I asked.

She tutted. "The research is iffy at best," she clipped, and then added, in a much softer tone, "Are you okay, though?"

"Yeah, I'm good," I lied.

"*Emory.*"

I guess I need to work on my skills of deception.

"I'm going to Thailand," I said decisively. "It'll be good to get away from here for a while."

Saying it aloud gave it more credence somehow. It *would* be nice to have a little change of scenery. Maybe a little change of me. After all, it was Emory James who had gotten himself here, who had blindly traipsed, if not down the aisle, then at least to the church with someone who had in the end found him lacking and made it a point to tell him so, in what was probably the most humiliating way possible.

I thought of Lisa Simpson, in that classic episode where she realizes she's not the shining star she thinks she is but actually a great big nerd with no real friends, and goes on summer vacation determined to become somebody else, somebody less of a loser. To make it stick, she takes an empty suitcase so she can fill it with new clothes for the new not-loser her.

It was too late for me to employ her brilliant empty suitcase trick, as mine had already been checked in, at a predictably exorbitant fee, but there was certainly a chance for a new not-loser me. I could be anybody I wanted; nobody in the entirety of Southeast Asia knew what I was like in actual life. I could be a different person every day if I so chose.

(Though I suspect that might be confusing after a while, and tiresome to the hotel staff.)

There was a lesson to be learned at the end of that episode, too, as I recall, about the importance of being true to yourself, but as I got off the phone with Linn, I decided I was going to be the kind of person who flouts the rules and laughs in the face of the morals of all stories. Insouciant, carefree, that's me, the new me.

Goodbye, Emory James.

Hello, um, also Emory James.

Well, it's not like I'm going to be changing my name; that takes a hell of a lot of paperwork, and I only just got this passport issued.

***

As it turns out, being a whole new you is a lot more difficult than expected when coming off a bout of international travel. I hadn't considered the fact that being stuck for seventeen hours at a ninety-degree angle in an enclosed space is not the most ideal of circumstances for someone who's only recently approached the beginner's level of affecting carefreeness.

I lumbered off the plane cranky, and, at baggage claim, veered sharply toward the stabby end of the irritable spectrum, as I suspected that the baggage handlers had conspired to hold my luggage back from the conveyor loop until the bitter end, for kicks and giggles.

When it did finally appear, I yanked it off the belt and trudged outside to find the shuttle bus that would ferry me to my hotel.

It was hot. Tropically, humidly hot. I couldn't remember why Michelle had decided to pick Thailand, and with each bead of sweat that emerged from my pores as I waited, I hated her more for it.

Being angry was probably better than being despondent, though. I had tried despondent the night before (or maybe two nights, depending on the time zone, which I hadn't yet worked out), all useless limbs and emptied out from crying. It hadn't been pretty.

It was in fact rather surprising that I had managed to roll out of bed at all, but spite had had a large role to play in it; Michelle was probably off doing a whole montage of pretentious New Yorky things with Good-Looking Bastard, and so I would counter it by splicing together my own clip show of tropical adventure.

I would have *fun* without her, by god. Fun and heatstroke. That would show her. That would learn her good.

The shuttle bus trundled in then, narrowly heading off my untimely death of drowning in a puddle of my own sweat. It was mercifully air-conditioned, its frigid current blasting the sweat off my face, which made me strongly consider becoming a religious votary to the bus.

By the time we reached the oceanfront island resort I was in considerably better spirits, and as I stood in line to check in I was presented with a glass of juice, adorned with a perky purple and white orchid.

See, I was having fun already.

"Good evening, sir, and welcome to La Celestia Resort," said the smiley man at reception when it came for my turn in line. His gold nametag, catching the light of the computer screen, read 'Alak'.

"Hi. Checking in. Emory James," I said, spelling my last name for good measure.

Fingers tapping with speedy efficiency on a keyboard, he pulled up the reservation, and then smiled some more. "Ah, Mr. James. You are here with your wife, yes?"

"Um," I said, looking away.

Michelle had done the reservations; she had probably told them we were honeymooning here, on the off-chance of getting some kind of reduced rate, or maybe an extra mint on the pillow as a reward for completing an assisted walk down the aisle.

"No... I-- No. No wife today."

Alak blinked at me. The smile was still cemented in place, but his eyes were confused at my perseveration and slightly panicky, unsure how much he could or should ask without overstepping his professional boundaries.

"She..." *Died?*

No, oh god, why would that even be the first thing I thought of? Of course I couldn't say that. What kind of an asshole would I be if my wife died and I went on vacation? Probably a felonious kind of asshole, if Investigation Discovery's regular programming is any indication.

"It's, uh, complicated," I said, hoping that would sufficiently cover it. Hey, it's good enough for my online social network, right? If two hundred of the closest people I regularly forget exist can accept such a statement, surely Alak wouldn't mind.

"Okay! No problem!" he said, a shade too brightly for my liking.

I sipped at my juice. My palate detected citrus and guilt, with a soupcon of self-reproach.

I had the feeling that had I been in top, life-changing form, I might have been able to convince Alak that the initial reservation for two had been some administrative mistake on their end -- no wife, no nothing, just a dashing young traveler out for solitary adventure, kindly update your faulty records, my good man. Wink, smile, we share a laugh, and I stride to my room fairly reeking of aplomb.

Instead, I was getting furtive glances from the clerk; he was probably wondering why I had shown up alone -- I mean, I'd wonder. A little spat, maybe? Or more like a series of little spats that had led up to a giant one? Or maybe she caught a horrible case of dengue fever elsewhere in these perilous tropics and he left her to wither alone. Or, oh my god, he stole this poor couple's identities and is on holiday on their dime!

"It didn't work out," I blurted, desperate to have him stop imagining my imaginary scenarios.

When New Year's next rolls around, I will resolve to watch fewer true crime documentaries on television and maybe also to look up my friendly neighborhood psychiatrist.

"Sir?" Alak said.

"Nothing, sorry," I mumbled.

He handed me my keys and wished me a pleasant stay, indicating with his palm which direction I was to go. Obediently, and glad to go, I left him to deal with a couple who had been waiting behind me, a couple who was probably normal and didn't show up to their honeymoon at half the original value.

The resort was a sprawling arena of pebbled walkways edged by lush, fragrant foliage that led to little villa-style rooms. The room itself was all dark wood and low lighting; pristine white towels that had been fashioned into a pair of swans greeted me from the edge of the bed, swimming in a scatter of fresh rose petals. It was all very romantic, so I undid both swans and hung them up by their former necks in the bathroom, and swept the petals into the garbage can.

A complimentary fruit basket sat on the coffee table. I selected a grape, my sustenance for the night. When you've been dumped, caloric intake seems largely unnecessary, as moping around expends little to no energy at all. But just to be on the safe side, I ate another grape, in case of emergency languishing. You never know.

They don't teach you these things in school, or in any extracurriculars. I'm fairly certain I can still write down at least half of the quadratic equation and tie a passable knot, but those skills don't come in handy often in the rest of your life. What the boys of America really need to be prepared for is how to deal with the sucker punch of heartbreak.

Try not to die of alcohol poisoning would likely be in the top five. I don't know the rest. If I did I might not have felt compelled to flee the country.

Left to digest my pair of grapes, I plodded around the room, checking out amenities I probably wouldn't even remember were available come morning.

A long shower later, I climbed under the crisp, cool sheets, and stared at the canopy above, alone but for the noise in my head.

Michelle would've loved this place. Which probably explains why she booked it to begin with. She would have cooed over the towel swans and made a note to learn how to fold them that way when we got home; she would have pressed a couple of the rose petals between the pages of her journal for remembrance's sake; she would've inspected the room with half a smile on her face and a long lock of chestnut hair twirled around her finger while it sank in that we were here, and married, and allowed free roam in paradise for a week.

It was strange how I could so clearly see all these quotidian things about her, as if she were right here with me, and yet the biggest leap of her life, running away from her own wedding, I hadn't seen coming at all. Did that make her unpredictable, or me stupid?

I thought I knew her. I thought I knew her passions in life, her calm under pressure, her weakness for salted licorice found only online. I had spent four years knowing her, from the first day of my first real job when I'd nearly cut her nursing rounds short running smack into her around a corner, to the mutually agreed upon date we would have been wed had someone better not come along.

I felt cheated. It wasn't supposed to work this way. All that time and effort and energy expended, all for nothing. Why, after all we had been through, was she the only one who got to be happy?

Misery climbed into bed with me, and I turned on the TV for better company. After a while, it sang me to sleep.

Chapter Two

It was fairly early when I shuffled out to partake of the hotel's complimentary breakfast, the last pink dregs of sunrise still straggling in the sky.

At this hour, an hour I witnessed only because jet lag wouldn't let me sleep through it, the restaurant was nearly empty.

An elderly couple sat at one table reading the paper, occasionally forking something on their plates when they remembered it was there. Besides them was a Japanese group of four seated in a corner of the restaurant, eager to get a head start on the day. As far as I could tell, they were two couples come on holiday together; one pair was holding hands underneath the table. I hated them on sight, and then felt bad about it.

Despite the previous night's dieting plans of eating nothing but my feelings, my stomach was being rumbly, so I dotted my plate with little samples of every hot breakfast item on offer to appease it, and headed to the outdoor dining area.

I was the only one out there and had my pick of tables, so I took one with a view of the beach. It had an umbrella in the middle, which was helpful, as my partially Scandinavian ancestry had long ago decreed it impossible for me and future generations to properly tan; we are blessed instead with the ability to hear ourselves sizzle under the sun, and then peel like elementary school glue.

No sooner had I settled myself in the wickerwork chair than I heard the telltale slap of somebody's flip-flops come to join me out on the patio.

European, I guessed. He was about my age, and lean, draped in a loose, white linen shirt and matching shorts. He clearly did not have the curse of a Scandinavian complexion on his head; he was one of those dark-haired, kissed-by-the-sun types, who swan around the continent on vintage Vespas, giving women the vapors.

I gave him a cursory nod in greeting as he sat down a couple of tables away with coffee and a bowl of fruit, and set my attention to eating my breakfast sampler in a spiral. Sausage, good. Eggs, so-so. Noodles, not bad.

"Cubs fan, huh?"

Startled, I glanced around, but there were still only the two of us out there, which meant he was talking to me. I must have given him a look of total confusion, not least because his accent was incongruously American, and he nodded meaningfully toward my chest.

"Oh," I said, catching a downward glimpse of my faded blue T-shirt with the large C logo in the middle. "Oh, yeah. Um, yeah. Since I was a kid."

He smiled with understanding. "I was raised on the Sox myself. I guess this means we're legally obligated to hate each other."

"Boo hiss boo," I said mildly to my new baseball-themed nemesis.

Despite the dire proclamation, he cradled his cup of coffee in one hand and came over to my table.

"Mind if I...?" he asked, his hand on the chair opposite mine.

I gestured a go-ahead, as it didn't seem as though I really had any other choice. I mean, what was I supposed to say? *No, go away. Stranger danger!* Besides, he was already sitting down.

He stuck out his hand. "Nate Harris."

I briefly flirted with the thought of giving him a fake name but couldn't come up with a reasonable one in time. I mean, true, there are lots of names for the taking, but you have to consider the fact that some people just don't make very convincing Tonys or Steves or Enriques.

On the momentous occasion of my birth, I was christened and thus doomed with an old man name, and my whole personality has molded itself around that name -- I am fussy and inflexible, I think today's children don't know the value of a dollar, the designated hitter rule is baseball's greatest travesty, and butterscotch candies are actually quite tasty.

"Emory James," I said, taking his proffered hand.

He had a nice, firm grip, of which I approved. There's nothing more deflating than meeting someone whose hand collapses in yours as if mustering the wherewithal to contract a few muscles for two seconds is just too much to bear.

"That's an interesting name," Nate said.

"Mm, my grandpa's."

"Do you take after him?"

I shrugged. "Old and crotchety? Absolutely."

Nate had an easy laugh, as though his face was made for it. "I don't know; you don't seem so bad," he said, with what could only be described, alarmingly, as a twinkle in his eye.

Oh my god, was I being flirted at?

No, of course not. Nobody flirts at me. It just isn't the done thing.

I thought I had been winked at once, across the high school gym masquerading as a crowded dance floor, but it turned out she had a mild tic. What a relief that had turned out to be.

It was then that I remembered I wasn't Emory, but New Emory, and New Emory was, as yet, a blank slate. Maybe New Emory *was* the kind of guy people casually threw pick-up lines at; maybe New Emory -- hereafter referred to as just Emory, because the more I say 'New Emory' the more it sounds like an East Coast town populated by crabby old Dutch puritans -- maybe Emory was the kind of guy who didn't seize up in flattered terror when anyone gave him a second glance that lasted longer than a glance.

Maybe Emory had it in him somewhere, deep down, to be a Good-Looking Bastard. Or at least a Not Unattractive Bastard. Ooh, or a Not Unattractive Bastard with Actual Heart of Gold!

Although, seems like if the Heart of Gold was actually Actual, that would negate the whole Bastard part.

Well, Emory probably wasn't the kind of guy who troubled himself with labels and technicalities; just went about his manly, enigmatic business of being a bastard, or not.

And also maybe Emory needed to stop referring to himself in the third person. I don't know how Caesar did it all the time; it's really weird. Maybe when you're emperor of Rome you're afforded a pretentiousness allowance. That might also explain why everybody was so eager to stab him, though.

"Maybe," I said smoothly. "But Aristotle once said that people with curly hair can't be trusted, so..."

Nate tilted his head, amused, or possibly befuddled. "Hm," he said, choosing to play along and scrutinizing me with narrowed eyes, "I'd ask you to confirm or deny it, but then I wouldn't be able to take your word for it, would I?"

"And therein lies the conundrum," I said, steepling my fingers.

"Well, you're a regular international man of mystery, then."

I glanced down at my ancient T-shirt again, and the black rubber flip-flops I'd bought for under three dollars decorating my feet. "Hm, between the two of us you seem the more likely candidate."

"Nah, it's always the ones you least suspect," Nate said, leaning back in his chair, casually resting one ankle over the opposite knee. "So I guess it would be pointless to ask you what you're doing in Thailand, huh?"

Was he fishing? He was fishing. Or making polite conversation. Or about to attempt to sell me a timeshare, the fiend.

"Is it too predictable to say that if I told you I'd have to kill you?"

"Little bit," he chuckled.

"In that case," I said, "I am a normal person on a normal vacation."

It wasn't too far from the truth; on good days I could pass for normal, and if you conveniently forgot, as I intended to for at least the next week, the circumstances that had landed me here, I was on a perfectly acceptable version of a vacation.

"Did you see the night market yet?" he asked. At my head shake, he added, "Oh, you should; it's fantastic. The food here is amazing."

"Duly noted," I said.

I was afraid for a small moment that he was going to ask me to come along with him, possibly so he could hustle me down a dark alley and divest me of my kidneys -- who knew with these friendly, Europeanly handsome types -- but instead he glanced at his watch and rose from the chair.

"Hey, man, thanks for indulging me with the small talk," he said, sticking his hand out again, and I had no choice but to take it again. We shook. "I've got to be somewhere. I'll see you around, maybe."

"Yeah," I said. "See you around."

Departing with a smile, Nate disappeared around the corner. Alone again, I pushed the cold remains of my breakfast around the plate with my fork, wondering what to do with myself.

I had come without any advanced planning. Michelle's the trip planner -- she has lists and top tens and maps; I just go along, driving if it needs to be done, taking pictures if she wants to be in them, occasionally deciding where to go for dinner to fulfill my quota of usefulness.

Now, left to my own devices, I was at loose ends. Maybe it was time to get that couples massage sorted out.

***

With Alak's assistance, I managed to flag down a local bus to take in some of the scenery -- a couple of temples, a street market and, after some Oscar-worthy miming on both my and the bus driver's parts, a postcard-grade beautiful waterfall a little bit off the beaten path.

The waterfall was tall and loud, but the white noise kind of loud people play at night so they can fall asleep. Things chirruped in the distance, invisible and bright. A small rainbow hovered amidst the spray of the waterfall as it cascaded onto the worn rocks at its base, a forty-foot drop from where I was standing.

A smallish tour group that had arrived before me left in a drove, happily packing their cameras, herded back to their van by an enthusiastic guide clutching an oversized plastic sunflower, and for the moment I was alone, presumably before the next tour group descended.

I stood precariously on one of the wet rocks to the side of the falls, peering over into its depths. A fine mist of water fleeted past my skin, and I felt as ancient as the ground it had staunchly etched away for millennia, and twice as weary.

A deep stretch of space stared up at me, and I wondered, for the briefest of moments, who would miss me if I simply disappeared over the edge.

It was a maudlin thought, and I stepped away.

For the sake of posterity, and to provide physical proof of actually being capable of having *fun* post-dump, I snapped a couple of pictures of the waterfall. It would have to do.

I trekked back out to the main road, and by some miracle, got on another bus that eventually dropped me off within walking distance of my hotel, by which time the sky was descending into an Impressionist's dream of muted orange and violet smears.

Back in my room, I took a quick shower; there was one indoors and one out, and I chose the latter, for its sense of adventure. It was the kind of thing the new me would do, I thought, even though I spent the entire time anxiously trying to discover chinks in the tall shrubbery that edged the shower stall, in case anybody was doing the same from the outer perimeter.

I guess the new me isn't cool with public nudity either.

Subsisting on the contents of the fruit basket for the night didn't appeal, and I didn't particularly want to spend ten million baht on room service or the hotel restaurant either, so I threw clothes on and went back out to brave more uncharted territory.

I was doing all sorts of new, un-Emory-like things today. It felt, if not good, then at least necessary.

Left to my own devices, I'd be content kicking around my usual few haunts for years, no matter what exciting new things sprang up around me. It had taken me two years to even go and see the Bean at Millennium Park after it was installed, and then only because a couple of old college friends were in town on holiday and I'd been appointed to show them around.

Out of nowhere, I thought about how proud Michelle would be of me for going out of my way to try something new, only belatedly remembering that she wouldn't even know it, that she wasn't even in my life anymore, except for what ties I couldn't cut in my head.

In one fell swoop she had cut all of hers with me, and it was hard to decide which was more upsetting -- that, for all the kindness and compassion she had made me love, she could do this so easily and quickly with no regard to my say in the matter, or that I still wasn't angry enough to want to let go. If she came back to me now, by some miracle, I'd probably give in. There would be some yelling and extractions of promises and obviously some kind of apology on her part, but I would take her back.

She had been my life for years, and now she was just gone. It was as though someone had simply come along and lopped off one of my limbs without provocation, and though I could see its clear absence, I could still feel its phantom there anyway, with a pain I could never hope to assuage because some part of my brain still hadn't figured out that that part of me didn't exist anymore.

Taking a deep breath, I stored her image away and walled it up, brick by brick. I wouldn't think of her crooked smile, or the bright amber eyes that never dulled even after a long day, or her capable hands, deft and dexterous even though they seemed so small in mine. Line by line, up and up went my wall. With a last slap of mortar troweled in, I put the final brick in place, sealing her out of my mind, like she had sealed me out of her life.

Satisfied, I released the breath, and carried on my way.

As I walked out of my room and past the restaurant, I remembered suddenly that morning's unexpected meeting with Nate, the potential organ harvester, and his tip about the night market. Market implied food, so I made a quick stop at the front desk to ask for directions and was on my way.

It didn't disappoint. Lit by street lamps, colorful lanterns and generators, the long street, blocked off from vehicles larger than motorbikes, was a riot of rich sounds and smells, most distinctly of deep-fried deliciousness. A light haze of smoke hung in the air from a hundred different cooking fires, stalls upon stalls of vendors hawking things I had never seen in my life, let alone put in my mouth.

Paralyzed by the sheer amount of choice, I bought nothing and instead kept walking and gawking, mentally keeping a list of all the things I might consider ingesting. A few vendors lacking in custom called out their wares, tried to catch my eye with wide smiles and friendly gestures as I moved past.

"Hey!"

I walked on, inspecting each stall's displays from a safe distance; get too close and I might feel obligated to buy up the whole street.

"Hey, Chicago!"

I paused. Weird.

A hand tapped my shoulder, and I turned. "Oh," I said, simultaneously glad to see an almost familiar face and worried that I was about to make a charitable donation to the organ black market. "Oh, it's you."

Nate grinned at me, somehow managing to dim the fluorescent light bulbs immediately adjacent to us. "Hey. Emory, right?"

"Yeah. Hey. Nate," I said. "What are you doing here?"

"I love this place," he said, radiating enthusiasm. "Different awesome thing to eat every night. Hey, have you eaten yet?"

"Ahh, no...?"

Probably should've said yes. I glanced around stealthily, making a note of all possible escape routes.

"Oh, man, you have to try this place," Nate said. He looked over to his left, getting on sneakered toes to peer over the heads of the crowd, even though he was taller than most everyone there. His face lit up as he spotted what he was looking for. "Yeah, there it is. Come on."

He took me by the arm and started walking us toward a stall, I didn't know which one. I looked at his fingers clasped around my arm as we moved through the throng. "Okay... So, this is happening..." I muttered to myself.

A thought suddenly occurred to him, and Nate stopped. It apparently wasn't to let go, however. He glanced at me somewhat warily. "Are you allergic to seafood or anything?"

"Um," I said, shaking my head. "Not that I know of."

"Excellent," he said, and pulled me along again.

I can't say why I didn't just shake him off; maybe it was the relief of having had a dinner decision made for me, or the sheer curiosity of finding out what was going to happen next. Nate was... interesting; he seemed like the kind of guy to which things happened that would then make incredible stories for dinner parties.

I was not that kind of guy. I moved through life carefully, always a few cautious steps behind the action, waiting and assessing. Maybe that was why I was tolerating Nate's exuberant charge tonight, to be something different.

We didn't end up too far from where we started, standing in line at a stall, behind a group of three girls. I leaned over to try to peek around them at what the stall was selling. There were things on a stick, which was about all I could make out, since the people in front were crowding around, and any signage available was all in Thai.

"What are you making me eat?" I asked.

As the group in front of us handed their money over and began moving away, Nate pointed to a stick in one of the girls' hands, atop which was perched something dark brown with char marks from the grill. "That," he said happily.

"Uh," I said. "That looks kind of like--"

"Baby octopus, yeah," he said, and gestured to the woman behind the stall that he wanted two.

I watched with trepidation the hawker retrieve two sticks from the front of her stand. "Wait," I said to Nate. "It just looks like a baby octopus or actually *is* a baby octopus?"

He smiled at the hawker, receiving the maybe baby octopi in a little plastic bag with red sauce at the bottom, and then turned the smile on me. "Which one is more likely to persuade you to eat it?"

"That is a great question," I said.

"It's really good, I promise," he said, though how he could have so much confidence in just to what extent our gastronomic tastes merged was beyond me. "Okay, if it helps, I'll go first."

He swirled the octopus on a stick in the bag, picking up as much sauce as he could, and then stuck the whole thing in his mouth, scraping it off the stick with his teeth. As he chewed, he made the kind of face celebrity chefs make when they taste whatever divine creation they have assembled in front of the cameras in under thirty minutes.

"That good?" I asked, skeptical. I couldn't recollect ever making that face when I'd had calamari before. They're kind of the same thing, essentially -- tasteless, rubbery cephalopods, and I said so.

Nate held the bag out to me, the remaining stick lolling around the mouth of the bag as he shook it lightly. "Just try it?"

He looked so earnest that I had to accede to his offer. "Okay," I said, sniffing experimentally at the sauce, "but if at the beach tomorrow I get attacked by a giant kraken for eating its beloved spawn, it'll officially be your fault."

With one hand on his heart, Nate proclaimed, "I promise I'll be consumed by guilt for the rest of my life. I will build a bronze shrine to your memory."

"Well, that seems pretty fair," I said, returning his smile.

Dunking the thing several times into its saucy surroundings, I did as Nate had done and ate the octopus in one go. It was smooth and chewy, and infinitely tastier than I'd imagined. I may have made the face, because Nate looked excessively pleased with himself.

"I see your point," I conceded.

He grinned. "Want another?"

"Kind of, yeah."

Emboldened by this culinary delight, I treated him to two more sticks and spent the next hour ambling up and down the street with him, looking for the next great thing to eat. Some were recommended by Nate, who, as I found out, had arrived three days before, and was therefore three days more experienced in the consumption of night market mysteries; others we dared each other to eat -- though eventually I had to draw the line somewhere, and that line was at anything with more than four legs (octopus notwithstanding).

As far as impromptu jaunts with somebody I barely knew went, it was surprisingly enjoyable and made me feel lighter than I had in days.

When we had eaten our fill of everything deemed worthy of our mad standards (the more unidentifiable the better), Nate and I walked back toward the resort, slowly, to aid digestion.

A gibbous moon hung neatly in the sky among a confetti of stars, and I stopped at the side of the road to look up. Back home, in the city, the nights are always so relentlessly, artificially bright, you don't get to see skies like this very often.

Nate stood beside me, craning his neck backwards. "Know your constellations?"

"Nah, only the Dippers," I said. I pointed up to a straight row of three stars, bordered at four corners. "And that one, Orion the hunter. I knew a bunch more when I was little, but those are the only ones that have stuck, I guess."

A breeze danced in, ruffling the treetops as it twirled past.

Nate glanced at me, and then jerked his head in the direction of our hotel. "Come on, I know where we can get a better view."

It probably says a lot about my self-preservation skills that it didn't occur to me not to trust him until we were halfway there, winding through the boughs of the resort and toward the beach it jutted up against. But then I guess I'd already mentally accused him of shilling timeshares and stealing innards today, so I'd met my quota.

There was a small handful of other people taking quiet walks along the wide stretch of shore, though for the most part the beach was ours.

Finding a spot that met criteria he didn't explain, Nate plopped himself onto the white sand and lay down, his hands cradling the back of his head. I sat a respectful distance next to him.

"See right there?" he said, stretching a finger toward the sky. "Where those three big ones make a triangle?"

"Yeah?"

He drew a line in the air between two of them. "Those ones are Altair and Vega. There's a cool Chinese story about them that I could bore you with if you'd like," he offered, grinning up at me.

I leaned backwards onto my elbows. "Hit me."

"Once upon a time, there was a beautiful princess," he said.

"Sorry, wait," I interrupted, waving a hand in his direction. "Did you mistake me for a seven-year-old girl? I mean, I know I'm not that tall, but--"

"Shut up," he laughed, and kicked sand over my foot. "Once upon a time, there was a beautiful princess from the heavens who weaved all the clouds in the sky."

She came down to earth one day and met a handsome young cowherd. They fell deeply and madly in love, and married, forging a simple but happy life together. Her parents were furious that she was consorting with a mere mortal and marched her back home; the cowherd tried to follow, but her mother carved out a river in the sky to keep them apart forever.

They live on as Altair and Vega, separated by the Milky Way, yearning for each other across the great divide. But once a year, their sad love story moves the magpies of the world to flock up to the stars and form a bridge so that the princess and cowherd may reunite.

"Well, that's romantic," I said grudgingly, thinking of how certain people formerly in my life could have learned something about the promise of commitment from these guys. "And also pretty depressing."

"All great love stories are," he said. "You know, your standard Romeo and Juliets--"

"*That*," I interrupted, "is a story about a couple of infatuated kids with poor communication skills."

Nate raised an amused eyebrow at me. "I didn't peg you for such a cynic, Chicago. Not a fan of love at first sight, huh?"

"I don't think it exists," I said, shrugging. "You do?"

He nodded solemnly. "Yup. To my great detriment," he said, a wry smile forming on his lips.

He didn't elaborate and I didn't ask. I mean, I'm just some dude he just met. Eating street food together isn't exactly a life-altering event that forges the kind of emotional bond necessary for kick-starting heart-to-hearts.

I wasn't sure I really wanted to know anyway. I mean, he's just some dude I just met.

We continued stargazing for a few minutes, the gentle lap of the ocean waves a backdrop to our silence.

I sat up with a grunt and brushed sand off my elbows. "Almost my bedtime," I said, by way of explanation.

It wasn't actually very late, and I had jet lag anyway, which probably meant I'd be staring up at the canopy of my four-poster until the wee hours, but if I didn't move now there was a good chance I'd stay out here until sunrise with Nate, if he didn't move either.

The idea of us, side by side, watching the stars glide across the sky wasn't unpleasant, but its very lack of unpleasantness was slightly discomfiting. I didn't know him, and there was no logical reason I should feel that comfortable with somebody I didn't know. And I didn't particularly want to contemplate it any further, so I got to my feet.

Nate made no move to follow suit, merely looked up at me from where he lay in the sand.

"Um," I said, feeling awkward, "goodnight."

He smiled. "See you around, Chicago."

Chapter Three

'Around' turned out to be the next morning at breakfast. Nate was already sitting out on the patio with an empty plate by the time I moseyed in. He waved when he saw me but gave no real indication that he expected me to follow in his footsteps from the day before and go and sit at his table to chat.

I dithered for a second. I suppose we were at least acquaintances now, and it would probably be rude to just sit somewhere else and not talk to him; at the same time, I wasn't sure if the nature of our acquaintance was such that my presence and idle chatter would even be welcome. I didn't want to be presumptuous, after all.

Hedging my bets, I took the table immediately adjacent to his. "Morning," I said carefully, setting my breakfast down.

"Hi," he said.

His wide smile assured me that I hadn't committed a heinous social faux pas, and I felt my shoulders ease. He picked up his coffee cup and, just as he had done the day before, came over to my table to sit opposite me, apparently suffering absolutely none of the same reservations I'd had about where we stood with each other on the friendly stranger scale.

"Sleep well?" he asked.

I made a side-to-side motion with my head. "Yeah, it was all right. Still fighting the jet lag a little," I said.

In fact, I hadn't been able to fall asleep until past two, idly flipping channels, once in a while landing on something I didn't mind passing the time with, but mostly thinking that I should have stayed on the beach a little longer, at least for the scenery. Television was so much less interesting that late at night, to say nothing of its paling in comparison to the panoramic view of the night sky.

"You?" I added.

Nate's face screwed up, abashed. "Kinda fell asleep on the beach for a bit. I wouldn't recommend it," he said, rubbing the back of his head. "Got a crick in my neck. And I woke up to a little sand crab heading up an expedition inside my shorts."

I couldn't help it; I laughed.

He shook his head, smiling behind the coffee cup he'd brought to his lips. "No sympathy at all. It's your fault, you know. You left me there."

"Okay, hey," I said, lifting my hands. "In my defense, I didn't think you'd be so useless out in the wild."

Nate shifted in his chair, relaxing into its back. "I thought I might rent a scooter and explore today. You want to come make sure I don't get eaten by wild dogs or anything?"

"Oh, uh," I said, slightly startled but, more distinctly, pleased at the invitation. Rather than talk myself out of it, I seized on the feeling and added, "Yeah, sure. But if there really are wild dogs, I'm just letting you know now that I'll be running. You're going to have to fend for yourself, buddy."

"You're a good friend, Emory," he said, facetiousness fairly dripping from his words.

"Yeah, I know. I try."

A corner of his mouth tilted upward. I'm not in the habit of making people laugh, but he seemed to find me endlessly amusing, and something about that made me want to try harder at it. For some reason, he thought my company enjoyable, and I wanted to be worth the thought.

He drummed a couple of quick fingers on the table, getting up from his seat. "Okay, I'll let you finish your breakfast in peace. Meet me by the entrance in half an hour, let's say?"

I nodded, and he flashed me a grin, walking off with his hands in his pockets, humming something identifiable only to himself.

Finishing up what I had left on my plate, I then drained my cup of Earl Grey and headed back to my room to swap out my flip-flops for sneakers. I grabbed my backpack, making sure all my travel essentials were safely tucked in there, and swung out the door again. If I didn't know myself better, I might even describe my footfalls as jaunty.

Nate wasn't at the hotel entrance yet when I got there, so I hung around, idly leafing through pamphlets near the front desk.

"Can I help you with something, sir?" the clerk at the front desk asked, when she noticed me taking and putting back several tourist brochures.

"Ah, no thanks. Just waiting for someone," I said, and she nodded in understanding, returning to her work.

"Hey," Nate called out, as he approached.

I secretly wished Alak was there to witness this. So I had arrived on the island with a wife conspicuously missing, what of it? I had a new *acquaintance* now, with whom I could get up to all kinds of shenanigans. Who needs a wife when you have a new best acquaintance? *Who indeed*, I would have demanded of Alak, so it was really for the best that he wasn't around to be party to my flirtations with madness.

"Touristy," I said to the large camera bag hanging from Nate's neck.

"Nah, it's kind of my job."

That wasn't too much of a surprise. Men like Nate who make ladies swoon on a regular basis usually don't tend toward staid occupations. They laugh in the face of the likes of accountancy and banking, and instead commandeer safaris, run Fashion Week and produce award-winning wines out of their own vineyards. They come in a packaged deal of exciting and ridiculous.

"Oh," I said, briefly imagining Nate hanging out of a Jeep, snapping pictures of a hungry hippopotamus intent on tenderizing him, "you're on assignment or something?"

Nate shook his head. "Not really. I'm trying to build up my portfolio a bit, see if I can get some good freelance gigs. Normally I do a lot of portraits and weddings, which is cool, but I kinda want something different." After a pause, he added, "But technically I'm just on vacation. Sometimes you just need to recharge, you know?"

"Yeah," I said, nodding slowly. "Absolutely."

As we walked out onto the main road, Nate said, "Mind if I ask what you do?"

"Speech therapist," I said. My degree says Speech-Language Pathology, but nobody ever knows what a speech-language pathologist is.

"Oh, cool. My niece is in speech therapy. Can't say her esses," he said, smiling at a memory I wasn't privy to. "How did you get into it?"

I've been asked some variation of this question approximately seventeen thousand times, mostly while I was in school. Meet anyone new at college and one of the first things they want to know about you is your major, and then all the explanations as to why. And then you meet new grad school classmates, and even though they have presumably gone through the same tiresome rote, they cannot stop themselves asking it all over again.

Being as personal as it was, I never liked telling anyone the real reason, and usually made one up, which was that I had been volunteering at a clinic and got interested in the discipline that way. Not totally untrue, because I did volunteer at a clinic, but only after I'd decided.

Maybe it was something in the bottled water, or maybe it was because Nate wasn't going to be secretly judging my dedication and worth as a colleague and future job competitor, but I felt no compulsion to keep the truth to myself this time.

"My grandpa had a stroke when I was fifteen. Oh, he was the one who taught me all about baseball," I added, remembering the similar history Nate and I had in being raised on the national pastime.

"Oh, yeah? He got you into the Cubbies?"

"Yeah," I said, smiling to myself, taking my turn now to indulge in the bits and pieces of remembrances that belonged only to me. "Every Sunday, we'd play catch in his backyard, and if the game was on TV we'd watch, and if it wasn't, we'd listen to it on the radio. He always let me sit in his La-Z-Boy."

"Sounds great," Nate said softly.

"It was. He was great," I said, winning the award for understatement of the year. "But, y'know, when he had his stroke, he had hemiparesis and his language was shot. He couldn't communicate anything he wanted, and it killed me that I couldn't help him. Eventually he started working with a speech therapist, and it got better, and that's how I decided what I wanted to do."

"I bet he's incredibly proud of you," Nate said.

I shrugged. "He passed away a couple of weeks before I started college."

"Hm, I'm sorry to hear that, man," he said. "But I'm going to stand by my statement."

It shouldn't have meant anything, coming from someone who had no real idea what my relationship had been with my grandfather, and what was essentially a pointless sentiment, but sometimes sentiment hooks a way into your heart before you can intercept it, so I left it there.

Our walk came to an end outside a scooter rental place, a small wooden hut with 'For Rent' signs staked into the ground. Flanked by the signs was a neat row of scooters in gleaming primary colors. I took a picture of them.

You hear of these stories in the news occasionally, a hiker who falls off the trail or gets eaten by a bear, and they accidentally take a picture of that last moment, leaving rescue parties to find and piece together the event from that final photo on the roll.

This was essentially the same concept; I figured that if anyone found my camera after I'd ridden, flailing, straight off a cliff, I'd be helpful and give them a clue. You know, just in case.

"Ever ridden one of these before?" Nate asked, inspecting a shiny silver scooter.

"Never," I said, snapping another picture for good measure and posthumous utility.

"Well, it's not too difficult; I can teach you," he said absently, smiling up at the rental representative who had come out of the hut to see what we wanted. "Do you have an international license, insurance?"

"Yes," I said decisively, though I could just as easily have lied to get out of riding on one of those things.

Michelle had delegated to me all the boring tasks of getting the proper documentation well before the trip, and it seemed just as well that I should use them after putting in all that work.

Besides, I wasn't allowed to be my overly prudent self this week, and as uneasy as it made me to think of plunging myself into what was frankly some of the craziest traffic I had ever seen, there was also a distinct sense of delight at the prospect of taking on, and possibly even succeeding at, something I had never considered doing before.

Nate grinned. "Well, then, we are going to have a fantastic day."

He bartered the rental price down, mostly by dint of charm, as far as I could tell, and put me in charge of taking several photos of the scooters we were renting in case of damage. I couldn't remember whether Michelle and I had planned to do this, and presumably we would've figured the process out eventually, or at least read up on it, if we were going to do scooters, but I was glad to have Nate's experience on hand.

After checking our tanks, doing a little trial run, and making sure the rental person had written down all the existing outer damage, Nate handed our money over.

"Okay," he said, squinting down the road. "There isn't really anyone around right now, so I think we can just have our lesson here?"

I shoved my helmet on, hoping it would hide the apprehension likely radiating from my face. "Sure."

It wasn't horrible, and nobody died in a fiery explosion, so I awarded myself a gold star. And, to his credit, Nate was a patient teacher, still in retention of his natural good humor by the end of the lesson about forty-five minutes later, when I'd finally gotten comfortable enough with the machine to be allowed in slow traffic.

We set off at a reasonable pace, taking quiet back roads where I couldn't accidentally run over or into anything.

The island, predictably, was pretty as its postcards made out, all turquoise waters and gleaming sand and generous hospitality. We made several stops along the coast, whenever Nate saw something that caught his creative eye. Not one to argue, I fished out my little digital camera as well at those points and took a few pictures of my own.

"Here," he said, holding out his hand for my camera at one of the beaches. "I'll take one of you. Otherwise all you'll have when you get back home to show everyone is scenery."

"Scenery's good," I said. "I mean, they know what I look like."

"Gimme." Nate took the camera from me and directed me to stand a little over to the left. "Okay, smile."

I did.

Nate lowered the camera. "Dude, I said smile."

"What? That's what I'm doing."

"No, you look like you're posing for your eighth-grade school photo. Stretching your mouth one millimeter to the left doesn't count as a smile."

I elevated an eyebrow. "Are you always this pushy when you take people's wedding pictures?" Dropping my voice an octave, I imagined him out loud, "*Hey, you, you guys are the worst at being in love. Why isn't my heart melting at the sight of you? I can't work like this.*"

Nate let out a bark of laughter. "What was that? I sound like I'm on a hellish cocktail of steroids and flu meds."

"That is exactly what you sound like," I said, shrugging to counterpoint the snicker that pirouetted out of my throat.

"*Smile*," he ordered, as he raised the camera again.

I did, maniacally.

The camera clicked, but I wasn't sure the picture would come out very well, given how much he was shaking with laughter at my stupid face, and watching him convulse set me off, too.

It was, all things considered, a pretty good day so far.

We hopped back onto our scooters once we managed to control ourselves, and rode on, checking out a temple on the way and a couple of tiny villages, eating things that caught our fancy and drinking out of coconuts as big as our heads.

As the day waned, Nate hurried us along back toward our resort so we could watch the sun say goodbye. We dropped off our rented scooters, incurring no extra charges thanks to Nate's careful inspections earlier that morning, and carried on toward the beach on foot.

"You've probably seen your fair share of sunsets in your life," Nate explained, as we followed the well-worn pathways of beachgoers before us, "but I promise you haven't seen one like this."

"Okay," I said, not all that excited about a sunset but going along anyway. He hadn't steered me wrong yet, after all.

I took off my shoes and socks the minute we hit the beach, the soft, warm sand filling the spaces between my toes with a luxurious welcome. We still had a little bit of time before the sun dipped beneath the waves, so we sat in silence, as we'd had the night prior, watching the sea approach and shy away again.

The sky was beginning to take on a pinkish hue, and Nate unpacked his camera happily. I scooped sand over my feet until they were buried to the ankles, and wiggled them out again, waiting.

As the sun began its descent in earnest, I saw Nate's point. If I had been better at science, I might have been able to articulate exactly what was happening up there, but all I could do was admire, slack-jawed, the sky in all its glory, purple clouds like shadows of uncharted islands in a bubblegum pink ocean.

"Holy crap," I said.

"Well said," Nate murmured, his face an intent mask as he alternated his gaze from the ocean and his camera's viewscreen.

Once her performance was over, the sun simply dropped out of sight underneath the waves, and dusk crept in with the evening breeze.

Nate lowered his camera and smiled at me. "Hey, thanks for coming out with me today."

"Oh, yeah, of course. Thanks for inviting me," I said, feeling suddenly awkward for no reason. "It was fun. It's nice to have a travel buddy."

The smile didn't leave his face, but he turned away toward the ocean again. For being so expressive, he was remarkably unreadable.

"Yeah," he said to the darkening horizon. "I'm glad we met."

"Me too," I said.

Something sweet and sour twisted in my chest. I couldn't find words for it; it felt like a first date I'd been on once, when we'd had an effortlessly great time and then we stood at her doorstep undoing it all while we said our goodnights, tangled up in indecision and faltering, nervous to go forward and reluctant to leave.

Was that what this was?

I was dancing on the edge of something new, though maybe not completely new, if I had to be honest with myself, and I wasn't sure what I would do if I fell, if falling was an option, if falling was something I was actually meant to do all along.

Afraid to find out, I scrambled to my feet as casually as I could to make my great escape. Nate looked up at me expectantly; I suspected I was getting very predictable.

"Think I'm going to have an early night," I said, not quite meeting his eyes.

"Okay."

What else could I expect? Did I want him to try to stop me? "Okay," I said, picking up my forsaken shoes. "Try not to fall asleep out here."

"Yeah, thanks," Nate chuckled softly. "I'll keep that in mind."

We bid each other goodnight, and I trudged back to my room with a mess of thoughts in my head too tight to unravel.

***

Acting is one of those talents I must've been asleep for while they were handing them out, relegated since my early youth to entirely expendable, sometimes made-up roles like Pine Tree and Villager #12 when school plays rolled around and the teacher was morally obligated to cast everyone in the room.

This breathtaking lack of talent had been discovered at our first-grade Nativity play, when, overtaken with anxiety as the spotlight swung onto my fake-bearded face, I lost the single line I'd been given, and improvised by bodily harrying Mary and Joseph off to the stage wings while shouting no at them. In all fairness, "no" was *one* of the words I'd been supposed to say.

I can only imagine what kind of lucrative, successful lifestyle I'd be leading now if I hadn't given the mother of God so much shit for asking if they could stay at my inn.

The following year, my bid at redemption as one of the Magi met with utter failure upon committing a similar faux pas, with even fewer words to say this time round, making it quite clear that I could never again be trusted on stage. My ensuing school years would thus involve being fourth alternate to the understudies of minor characters and pulling curtains for the children less inclined to contract retrograde amnesia on contact with theatrical glue.

That said, if ever you need someone to play the part of Forlorn Idiot, I'm your man.

This explains why I sat on the patio at breakfast, drinking my tea in slow motion for the better part of two hours.

It was pointless trying to convince myself that I wasn't doing it solely because I was hoping Nate would show up again and we'd go and have ourselves another adventure, at the end of which I'd probably scurry off again in typically maladroit fashion. But I didn't have to this time, because he didn't come.

There was a measure of relief at that, but it was largely drowned out by disappointment.

What had I expected, anyway? Just because we'd met at breakfast twice in a row didn't make it a routine.

And it wasn't like he owed me anything; neither of us had made any overtures at definite plans, nor was it reasonable of me to expect him to keep letting me trail alongside him while he navigated all the back streets and open road. We were simply fellow travelers who'd met by chance, and there was no rule that said we had to stick together, even if I kind of wished there was.

Nate was fun, and a real joy to be around. There are friends you have sometimes of whose company you never tire, no matter how much time you spend with them, and I had a feeling that Nate was that kind of friend, if we were actually friends.

Tipping the dregs of my tea past my lips, I decided that I was done waiting and to get on with my life. I was in Thailand, for god's sake; I could moon over someone all I wanted back home, not when I was halfway across the world with things to do that I'd never get to do otherwise.

One of those things was to get a Thai massage, for a single person, which I'd finally sorted out with the in-house spa, and tacked on all kinds of extra things involving hot stones and seaweed, on the reasoning that it was something I'd never normally do.

It passed a couple of hours at least, and I emerged from the spa freshly pink and pliable, and covered head to toe in essential oils. I smelled lovely.

I strolled back to my room to shower it all off, pretending not to be keeping a peripheral eye out for Nate-shaped passersby as I walked through the resort.

With nothing else on the docket, and feeling sleepy after the whole massage experience, I headed out to the beach to while away the rest of the day, making sure to douse myself in sunscreen beforehand.

Half a novel went by, as I sprawled under the shade of a helpful palm tree, and soon I was reading only by the light of a fading sun. I set the book aside, drawing my knees up to my chest. The sunset was different this time, burning the sky a deep orange. It was still beautiful, and I took my requisite picture of it, a souvenir of a lazy, unremarkable day.

Something about it, about my solitariness, incited a bout of restlessness in me, and I abandoned the beach in search of something to assuage the tension.

I walked the nearby streets, passing through the area where hawkers were setting up for the night market. It wasn't totally dark yet, the street lamps still waiting for their chance to shine. I followed their trail, ending up on a row of busy restaurants and bars.

Competing rhythms of techno and house music blasted from several establishments, and their neon lights highlighted in Technicolor the stumblings of the recently drunk as they weaved from one bar to the next.

I turned around, not wanting to be a part of that crowd, resigned to a quiet night in my hotel room with a passable movie on TV if I was lucky.

"Chicago!"

Warmth flooded my chest so quickly it nearly burned. I whipped my head around, but Nate was nowhere to be seen.

I searched my surroundings, emitting a small, chagrined "oh" to myself, as I realized I was in the near vicinity of a sports bar that catered almost exclusively to foreign tourists. It had several large-screen TVs mounted on its walls, one of which, closest to the street, was showing a tape delay of an American baseball game. A couple of Sox, tiny on the screen in their pinstriped whites, rounded the bases to a massive home run. It was too early in the season, just about a month in, to tell where all the chips would fall, but anything that put runs on the board was worth a cheer.

And now that I thought about it, whoever had cheered hadn't sounded like Nate at all.

Embarrassed, even though it was likely nobody even saw me attempt to give myself whiplash, I shuffled away from the bar and back the way I came.

I passed through the night market again, now in full swing, and stopped to buy a coconut waffle with which to distract myself from feeling things.

It didn't work; a few stalls down the row Nate was buying something inevitably tasty, and the thrill in my chest sparked up again in full bloom. I couldn't decide whether to spend the next few seconds trying to tamp it down or simply laugh at myself, at this night, ridiculous both.

Momentarily rooted to the ground, I watched as Nate came away from the stall, pleased with whatever he'd just purchased, poking at the contents of his Styrofoam container with a plastic fork. I chewed my waffle and waited, rocking on my heels while people weaved around me.

A slow smile spread over Nate's face when he spotted me, and we met somewhere in the middle of the distance between us.

"Hey, man," he said, and we did that dumb fistbump thing guys do when we can't articulate sentiments like *How lovely to see you again*. He peered at my waffle. "What've you got there?"

I traded a bite of my waffle for one of his green mango salad, and for a moment all was right with the world. I did mention I was ridiculous?

We roamed the street together again, buying more sweets, as he regaled me with all the cool things he'd seen that day out snorkeling; it sounded exactly like one of those tourist brochures from the hotel's front desk come to life, crystalline waters and exotic fish, swaying anemones and delicate coral. I kind of wished I had gone too. But mostly I wished I had gone with him.

"You want to grab a beer?" he asked suddenly.

"Sure," I said, always happy at the prospect of beer.

We turned toward the end of the street where I'd had my episode, and I resolutely ignored the sports bar that had unwittingly stolen my identity for a second. Passing up some of the louder bars, we ducked into one that seemed better suited to the temperament of the handful of tourists not particularly keen on blacking out in the street later on.

A few ladyboys were milling around at the entrance, chatting and laughing among themselves. On sighting us, a couple of them fluttered their fingers in our direction. I nodded politely, and Nate must have smiled at them or something, because it set them off giggling.

Once we were ensconced inside and seated at the bar, Nate said, "Oh my god, did you see the one in red?" He glanced furtively toward the entrance. "I used to date a guy who looked exactly like her."

I swiveled on my barstool a quarter-turn and leaned away from the bar, trying to get a better look.

Nate clouted me on the shoulder. "Don't stare," he laughed.

"What, you think it's him?" I said, squinting toward the ladyboy sparkling in crimson sequins while Nate ordered our beers. "Quite the looker."

"Yeah, well, I've always had excellent taste in men," he said.

He smiled serenely at me as he said it. I wasn't sure what to do with it, inordinately relieved when our beers appeared, scattering the rabble of butterflies that had taken up residence in my stomach. The ones that staunchly clung to my insides I'd drown with alcohol.

We made it through two large bottles each, spending most of our time people-watching, making up stories about their lives, once quietly cheering to ourselves when the ladyboy in red scored a shy, curious customer.

When almost everyone in the bar was given their backstories, and in some cases, macabre futures involving hair loss and dental crises, we decided to call it a night. I was pleasantly warm by this time, the fizz of the beer making it all the way to my fingertips.

The air outside was humid, intangible until it formed a film of moisture on my skin, and it was a welcome change when cool raindrops began to patter all around us.

Gradually, more of them came to join their fallen brethren, and we picked up our pace, though not quickly enough. Without warning, somebody upstairs flipped a switch, and the rainfall turned into a torrent, drenching everyone in its way within seconds.

"What the hell?" Nate laughed, looking up at the sky.

"Mandatory wet T-shirt contest," I called out, though nobody paid me any attention, thank goodness.

Laughing like children but too old to jump in puddles, we ran to the shelter of a row of closed shophouses near our hotel to wait out the rain. Other people scurried by, slapping splashes of water into the air as they passed, opting to run to wherever they were going rather than taking refuge as we did. Maybe they knew something we didn't, maybe the downpour would last for hours.

We waited quietly for a few minutes, squeezing what water we could from our clothing, watching sheets of rain soak the earth. The streets gleamed, a pretty canvas of reflected street lamps and traffic lights.

I leaned against a narrow wall and Nate came with me, the side of his arm flattened against mine. I didn't mind; it was warm.

And I didn't mind either when our hands bumped against each other and our fingers tangled, nor did I mind when Nate turned and slowly, cautiously pressed his lips to mine.

My intestinal tenants emerged in full force, flapping a tiny hurricane of exhilaration into existence. It spiraled in my chest and danced down the length of my spine, and its momentum swelled me toward Nate, sealing our mouths together.

It was different, and different in a way that made me feel as though everything before this point had been a little askew, a little off-center, but now I was righted, here in this rain, here with Nate.

It occurred to me then, a sudden spike of sourness in this resplendent haze, that I should mind the fact that I didn't mind any of this at all.

I couldn't blame it on alcohol; I've been drinking long enough to know when the point of drunken unreality takes over, and this wasn't it. This was purely me, and I had no idea what I was doing or whether I could cope with what my unknowing might lead to.

After all--

"My fiancée left me," I blurted, "on our wedding day. Four days ago."

Nate straightened, his head tilted toward me as though he needed to hear it again. "Oh," he said, blinking. His hand, splayed on my chest, moved up to rake through his hair, taking its warmth away with it. "Well, shit."

"Sorry," I mumbled. I scrubbed a palm over my face, weary of myself. "I guess I should've said something earlier."

"No, no, it's-- it's fine. I mean, it's not something you'd really discuss with a guy you've only known for three days, right?" Nate said. His words were accompanied by a shaky laugh, but it clearly didn't belong in the conversation.

The rain had slowed considerably now, as though each raindrop was taking its time on its way down so it could stare at the trainwreck of my life as it passed by.

"Sorry," I said again, not entirely sure what I was apologizing for this time, or to whom.

"What do you want to do now?" he asked.

I sighed. "I don't know, man. I-- I don't know."

Nate gazed out into the street, where the remnants of the downpour were dripping off trees and streetlights desultorily. "Come on, let's walk."

He said nothing for the rest of our sojourn back to the resort, just stuffed his hands in his pockets while we walked side by side, letting me process whatever thoughts I needed to process.

We reached a fork in the pathway leading to the hotel rooms, and Nate took his hands out of his pockets, clutching his room key in his right.

"I'm, uh, going this way," he said, jerking a thumb in the opposite direction of my room.

"Okay," I said. "Goodnight."

"Night," he said.

He hesitated, pebbles jostling against one another underneath his feet, and then took a step forward, wrapping his arms around me in a reassuring hug, which made me feel worse than if he had simply slapped me in the face for whatever it was that I had done.

Had I been leading him on all this time? Certainly not intentionally; he was someone I just liked being around, hanging out with. He was someone I just... liked.

Nate clapped me on the shoulder, a sideways smile on his face. "See you around, Chicago," he said, and spun on his heel and walked away.

I watched him get swallowed into the distance before heading toward my own room, wet and squishy and a complete mess from the inside out.

Chapter Four

When people tell you that things look better in the morning, you should consider severing ties with them immediately, because they are lying to your face.

The only thing that definitively changed between the night before and the light of the morning sun was that I was drier. Which was nice, but I would've also appreciated being less confused. No amount of sunshine would help me be less me.

I showered and dressed slowly, unable to stop myself thinking about Nate, about kissing Nate, about how laughably cliched it was, the big romantic kiss in the rain -- someone definitely needed to make a movie about me. But then, if it was a movie, someone would have yelled cut long before Jeremy Renner-me had the chance to word-vomit all his baggage.

If it was a movie, the kiss would be the end of it, and we'd all leave the theater happy in the knowledge that Emory and Nate go on to lead deliriously happy lives filled with quippy banter and hot sex.

My insides tightened lushly into a corkscrew at the thought, and I resolved never to think of Nate and sex in the same sentence again.

I considered skipping breakfast, afraid to run into Nate, afraid of how much anticipation I'd harbor if I went and he wasn't there.

But I was supposed to be a better version of myself here, for at least this one week; I had come, fueled by spite and defiance, resolved to find the means to be the kind of person who could look heartbreak in the face and remain standing. And that kind of person wouldn't be afraid of a little continental breakfast.

Mustering up what little courage I had in reserve, I stepped out into the sun and went to get me some eggs.

He was there.

Our eyes met, and his eyebrows lifted, the mild expression on his face telling me that the ball was entirely in my court. I scooped it right up and strode over with my breakfast to his table, leaving my apprehension to tumble, anchorless, in the wind at my back.

"Hi," Nate said, and I got the feeling that the only reason his smile wasn't wider was that he was trying very hard not to let it. At least, that's why mine wasn't.

"Hi," I said.

"Well," said Nate, kicking out the chair opposite him so I could sit, "what do you want to do today?"

"Anything," I said, meaning it in that moment. We could sit here all day drinking lukewarm coffee and I'd be wholly content.

Nate nodded. "Okay. You wanna get scooters again and hit up the places we didn't see last time? I could take more pictures of you looking like a serial killer to show your friends and family when you get home."

That also sounded lovely.

"Yeah, if by serial killer you mean international male model superstar, then yes."

"Of course that's what I meant," he said, nowhere close to placating, and not being at all stealthy about sneaking a strawberry off my plate.

I pointed my butter knife at him, choice weapon of the serial killer about town. "You're on thin ice, buddy."

Nate rolled an insouciant shoulder, letting my empty warning slick right off. "Nah, you'd be caught within days. Those nice people over there are going to remember that I was last seen with you."

I followed the line of his gaze to where a group of young holidaymakers were tucking into their breakfasts with avid enthusiasm, paying absolutely no attention to us. "What's to remember? They haven't even noticed the both of us staring at them."

It was the perfect set-up, though I didn't realize it until Nate was out of his chair and leaning over me.

"This," he said. With his hands on either side of my face, Nate bruised a kiss to my lips.

Where last night's kiss had been tentative and curious, this one knew exactly what it was doing, and what it was doing was lighting a white fire inside me that burned its way from my core to the tips of my nerve endings.

And fuck, but if it wasn't fantastic.

After an eternity that managed to condense itself into what must have been only a matter of seconds, Nate pulled away, the light in his eyes playful and a little bit smug. He patted my left cheek twice, as if to jolt me out of catatonia, which I might have normally found an unfair presupposition, but it turned out that I kind of needed it, because I didn't even remember having stood up or circling my arms around him.

"Yup," I said, once I remembered how to form words. "That-- that leaves an impression."

Nate laughed softly, and I kissed him again, for the hell of it.

One of the girls at the other table did a "Whooo!" at us, and while I slowly shriveled up and died of embarrassment, Nate inclined his head toward her to acknowledge her approval.

"You guys are so cute together," our personal, one-woman cheerleading squad offered without provocation.

"Oh, thanks," Nate said, beaming, his fingers playing with the back hem of my shirt.

We chatted with the affable group, all Australians, for a few minutes, trading tips on what things to see and places to avoid. They invited us along on a day trip they were taking to another of the nearby islands, but Nate graciously declined for the both of us.

Once they left, we sat down again and Nate leaned forward conspiratorially. "We're *cute* together," he announced.

"In all fairness, I think that's mostly down to you. I'm just happy to be here."

Nate made a face at me. "Come on, I wouldn't have started flirting with you if I didn't think you were cute. Better than cute."

"Oh," I said, pausing with a fork of pineapple halfway to my mouth, "you really were flirting that day? When we first met? I didn't-- I can't tell these things."

"Yeah," he laughed. "I was definitely flirting. I noticed you right off the bat, and I said to myself, 'Self, you will regret it forever if you don't talk to him.' So I did."

"Huh," I said.

Nate cocked his head, his eyes narrowing. "You don't believe me, do you?"

I shrugged, making a noncommittal sound.

"Emory," he said sternly, "you're a very handsome young man."

"Well, now you just sound like my Aunt Catherine."

"Who is apparently a brilliant woman," Nate countered. He held up a hand to shush the clever rejoinder on the tip of my tongue. "We will discuss this no further. This court rules that Emory James is a comely young gentleman of stainless repute, and any indications otherwise will be subject to penalties by law."

It was my turn to narrow my eyes at him in bemusement. "You have problems."

"Yeah, well, you have a nice face," Nate said mildly.

I considered this for a moment. "This is unwinnable, isn't it?"

He nodded solemnly. "For you, yes. If you surrender now," he offered, "I won't go into raptures about how your eyes sparkle like the ocean on a clear day."

"Jesus Christ," I said.

Nate flashed me a grin, his foot hassling my shin persistently underneath the table. "I'll do it, man; don't think I won't. And I'll do it in front of people, too."

"You're ridiculous, you know?"

"And *you're*--"

"Okay, okay, okay." I waved my hands in front of his face. "I'm everything you say that I am and more, you weirdo. Will you shut up about my face now?"

He folded his hands neatly in his lap, his work done. "Yes. Now, eat up, there are escapades to be embarked upon."

In an attempt to get the last word in, I bounced a red grape off his head.

Nate narrowed his eyes. "That was uncalled for. This isn't a high school cafeteria, you know; you can't just start food fights whenever you feel like it."

"That's exactly the kind of talk I'd expect from someone with no ammunition," I said airily, plucking another grape from the bunch and lobbing it carelessly at him.

He tried to snare it out of the air with one hand but fumbled it, and it ended up squishing in his hand. He laughed, grabbing the napkin next to my plate to wipe off the juice, and tossed the used napkin at me.

"Wager," he said. "Next three grapes I will catch in my mouth."

"What if you don't?"

"Does it really matter?"

Agreeing that it didn't, we spent the next ten minutes laughing like idiots trying to throw grapes into each other's mouths from increasingly greater distances. The other people scattered about the restaurant would definitely remember us.

After a particularly skilled toss on my part, we left the table to go in search of scooters, ending up at the same rental place we'd gone to the first time. Now that I was sufficiently experienced in scooting, we took off with a minimum of fuss, a warm island breeze and the occasional bug on our faces.

Between the two of us we decimated the local supply of young coconuts by drinking about three thousand of them everywhere we went, pausing in our wanton destruction only to devour street food on sticks and photograph them beforehand, if we remembered.

By late afternoon we rolled up to a beach park the Australians had recommended to us, equal parts stunning seashore and lush vegetation. Nate unpacked his camera as soon as we parked and locked our scooters, indecision all over his face as the panorama unfolded itself to him, unable to even pick a place to start shooting.

I liked watching him at work, his intensity and passion out for all the world to see. He framed his pictures with careful precision, always aiming for the angle that gave him the best light. He'd shown me some of the photos he had taken today on his camera viewscreen, and though I'm not exactly a connoisseur of the fine arts, he was definitely wasted on the matrimonial services he usually did.

I left him to do his thing and eased myself onto the grass, drinking in the scenery. It was the kind that made people seriously consider leaving their jobs and lives. I could see the allure -- out here, even with the other tourists milling around, it was unbelievably serene; looking out onto the ocean felt like you were staring into glittering blue swathes of forever.

Plus, the coconuts were plentiful and delicious.

Nate ambled over eventually, juggling a variety of lenses as he reorganized his camera bag. "Hey," he said softly, and offered a hand to pull me up.

I resisted the urge to yank him down instead, and rose to my feet, brushing loose grass from my person. "Get what you wanted?"

"Yeah," he said. "Great view."

He held his hand out again, palm up this time.

"What?" I said.

"Portrait of a serial killer?" he said. "Sorry, I mean, portrait of a chiseled serial killer."

"Smirking doesn't become you," I said loftily, though I put up no additional resistance and surrendered my camera to him.

While he talked me through the basics of smiling, I wondered if I should ask to take a picture of him as well, for future reminiscences' sake. What we had here couldn't last; I'd remember it fondly, but it wasn't a forever kind of thing, and we both knew it.

It wasn't totally ideal, but I could live with it. After all, I'd tried the whole till-death-do-you-part thing with someone once, and what a spectacular failure that had been. Maybe it was just better to go with a till-vacation-ends-or-you-run-out-of-money-do-you-part plan. Nobody would find you pitiful then, just cavalier.

Besides, I could go only so far with being somebody new. Vacations were all well and good for trying something different, but once I returned to all the trappings of my real life, there wouldn't be room for a new me. Whether I was old or new, I still had to deal with being dumped, being pitied, and being sad and occasionally thinking I would die alone. There was no way I could change myself enough to not be any of those things.

This, here, was just a one-off, a respite from myself. This wasn't really me, but I'd enjoy not being me while I could.

"You know, showing your teeth is a sign of aggression in chimps," I said, being a willfully intractable pupil.

He arched a single eyebrow at me, obviously unimpressed with my fine grasp of simian trivia. "And you just compared yourself to a chimpanzee."

"Yeah, well, you're the one who's attracted to me, so I think I'm the one who comes out on top in the end."

Nate laughed. "You're an idiot."

"Again," I said complacently, "you're the one who likes me."

He let out a loud, long-suffering sigh, theatrical, resigned to his fate. "I do like you."

"Yeah?" I said, spreading my arms open, littering gauntlets everywhere with impunity. "What are you gonna do about it?"

"I," Nate declared, "am going to make you smile."

He sauntered toward me in a manner that would probably be outlawed in some of the more conservative countries, his eyes hooded and dark as he stood with his face mere inches from mine. Our lips brushed briefly, barely a touch at all, but it still sent a frisson running through my veins.

"You can't do this every time you want me to agree with you, you know," I said, with what I thought was a valiant attempt at equanimity.

"I know," he said, and, out of nowhere, poked me in the side.

There was a loud squawk, which I am prepared to swear in front of a jury of my peers did not come from me, and I jumped away, laughing.

"Yes!" Nate crowed, pointing a victorious finger at me. "I knew you'd be ticklish."

"Wow," I said, rubbing my side. "That was low. Like intentionally hitting the batter low. You're going to pay for that, Harris. Maybe not today, maybe not tomorrow, but *soon*. I shall have my revenge."

"I look forward to it," he said brightly.

We strolled around a little bit more, mingling around some of the other park visitors, and he managed to get a proper picture of me, without me making a gargoyle face and without him harassing me about doing it wrong.

As we inspected the last picture, a middle-aged woman who had been standing nearby asked, "Would you like me to take one of you both?"

"Oh. Uh," I said.

"Yeah, that would be great," Nate filled in, handing my camera to her.

She made the universal gesture for *Stand closer together*, and I squished into Nate's side, my arm slung loosely around his shoulders, while his snaked around my waist, resting his hand at my hip.

When she passed the camera back, Nate fumbled with his bag strap and unhooked the camera bag from his neck. "Would you mind taking another one on this one, too?" he asked.

As he explained to her what to do on his vastly more complicated camera, I smiled to myself, pleased to know that I'd be a part of his future reminiscences as well.

We took the picture, and Nate checked the viewscreen. "Perfect," he murmured. "Thanks."

The woman smiled and gave us a friendly nod, going on her way.

Having absorbed our fill of paradise, Nate and I went back to get our scooters, and rode leisurely back toward base camp, stopping once along the way for a dinner of the cheapest and tastiest seafood I'd ever had the pleasure of stuffing my face with.

Once we dropped off our scooters, we headed toward the beach again, settling down at what I had dangerously begun to think of as *our* spot. Taking its cue, a sand crab scuttled away at our approach, vanishing into its burrow.

I dug my toes into the sand. We'd missed the sunset, but the ocean at dusk had its own enigmatic charm.

"So, um," said Nate, uncharacteristically diffident. "My flight leaves tomorrow morning."

Even though I knew this would come, at some point or another, something in my chest still coiled tightly, unpleasantly. "Oh," I said.

Nate trailed a finger along the length of my forearm. "I'm sorry I didn't say anything sooner, but I didn't want to have it hanging over our heads all day, you know?"

"Yeah," I said. "Yeah, I get that. I'm leaving in a couple of days too, anyway."

Now that it had come to it, saying goodbye was a lot harder than I'd thought it would be. How had I become so attached to a person in less than a week?

Nate looked at me. "What do you want to do?"

For all my intentions at being anyone else but me, I couldn't leave this to anyone *but* me. Practically speaking, I still knew next to nothing about Nate -- other than what we did for a living, we'd managed to exchange little personal information; I didn't know where he was from, or where he had grown up, or what his family was like, or his favorite color.

What all this boiled down to was simply a summer fling. Well, a slightly off-season fling since it's cheaper to fly during non-peak times, but still -- it was just a fling. A spectacular fling, as flings go, but never meant to last.

Of course I liked him now, but we were also on vacation, responsible for no one and nothing, free to do as we pleased. Vacation is nothing like the real world; that's why we take them, to indulge in the fantasy of not living out our life choices for a little while.

We were both headed back to our real worlds soon; I didn't know what his was like, but mine included returning unopened wedding gifts and letting voicemail defend me from pitying phone calls.

It was all very sensible in my head, though saying it out loud made no sense to my heart.

Neither of us had room in our lives for this kind of attachment, and we agreed to leave whatever we shared here, just let it be what it was.

"But we still have the rest of today," I said, some delusional, hopeful part of me insistent on dragging out the inevitable.

Similarly afflicted, Nate nodded and said, "We do."

What little distance there was between us disappeared in a split second, the both of us turning at the same time, our bodies meeting in the middle, our mouths melting into each other's, our heartbeats pounding to the same desperate rhythm.

If all we had left was the vestiges of this night, then we might as well make it count.

Above us, the deepening sky sparked its stars to life, and we watched them shine for a moment before rising to our feet, fine dustings of sand falling away from us.

Silently we walked through the resort grounds, and when we came once again to the forked pathway that diverged toward our rooms at opposite ends of the hotel, we turned in the same direction this time.

***

It seems maudlin to say that my holiday experience pretty much ended the moment I waved goodbye to Nate as he boarded his shuttle to the airport some short hours later, but let's call it like it is.

I spent my last two days there not even trying to pretend I was up for wrangling a solo adventure, and just bummed around the resort, my listlessness seemingly tangible within a mile-radius; Alak looked concerned at me and offered to help me book a relaxation massage.

Just to have something to pass the time, I let him. It seemed to cheer him up.

When the time for my departure rolled around, I couldn't decide whether I was happy to leave or not. On the one hand, I was beginning to irritate myself with my incessant expectation of seeing Nate pop up everywhere; on the other, I was going back to my normal life as Emory, he of failed weddings and even worse receptions.

Still, happy or not, I left Thailand behind and got on a plane home.

A million hours later, having thoroughly enjoyed the vocal stylings of two distressed infants on each flight and probably the worst movies ever committed to film, I opened the door to my empty apartment, and a sigh shuddered out of an equally empty me.

Sadly, the pile of wedding presents hadn't miraculously vanished in the night. It's so typical of the fine china dishes you registered for not to run away with any of the matching cutlery when you want them to.

Having left my cell phone turned off while away, I retrieved it from the inside pocket of my carry-on and sank onto the couch to check my messages. Too tired to even contemplate holding the phone up to my head, I played the messages on speaker.

One by one, I listened to them, one from my mother, another from work. I stared at a blank wall, simply letting the sound waves filter around me and out of my way, until the next message came on.

"Hey, Em." Michelle's voice filled the space of my living room, and when it had nowhere else to go, kicked me in the stomach. "You're not picking up your phone... Um, I don't blame you, but I want to say that I'm really sorry about, um, the wedding and everything. I know it was--"

"--Message erased," said my loyal voicemail. "Next message."

"Hi, Em," said Michelle again. "Um, I don't know where you are, and Hal's obviously not talking to me right now, but I wanted to make sure you're okay? It'd be-- It'd be nice if we could still be friends. Call me when you get this, okay?"

No, thank you.

I went through the rest of my cell phone messages and deleted all the ones she'd left without listening to any of them in their entireties, feeling sick.

Leaving the wedding gifts alone for another day, I rolled my luggage into the bedroom. I had intended to unpack like a responsible adult but ended up shoving it against one bedroom wall. It could wait.

I showered and crawled into bed, tired all the way to my bones. Maybe when I awoke, seven years would have passed, and I'd wake up to an Emory who had his life together.

Chapter Five

I had to Google the proper etiquette for dealing with the wedding gifts. It wasn't much, but if I was going to be a poor schmuck dumped at his own wedding, at least I wouldn't be a poor schmuck with no manners on top of it.

I also resolutely did not Google 'Nate Harris'.

Since I was on the computer anyway, I thought I might as well upload my photos now or I'd never get around to it. One by one, they appeared on my screen, beach after beach, golden temples, wide spans of coconut trees. They all seemed so distant now, like someone else had gone and taken those pictures in my stead.

The picture of me and Nate on our last day came up, the only one of the two of us together, and I pretended it wasn't the reason I'd gotten my camera connected to the laptop before doing almost anything else.

It was a good picture. You could tell by the amount of time I spent staring at it.

Someone pinged me on Skype, and I jumped, startled out of my mooning. I'd forgotten that I was automatically signed in. It was Linnea, and although I didn't really want to talk to anybody at the moment, or for the next millennium, give or take a century, I accepted the call anyway. I'd catch hell otherwise.

"Hey, friend," she said warmly. "You made it home."

"Hey," I said.

"Are you tired? Is this a good time?"

She was tiptoeing around eggshells; normally she'd have barreled right through to whatever she wanted to talk to me about by now. From where my laptop's webcam was situated at the dining table, she could probably see some of my living room landfill, where good gifts go to die.

"Ah, yeah, it's fine," I said, figuring I might as well start getting used to real life again. "And you don't have to be extra nice to me about the whole wedding-falling-apart thing. I'm totally over it."

"My darling, you're the worst liar I've ever seen."

"Yeah," I agreed.

"We don't have to talk about it, though, if you don't want to," Linn said. She made an effort to perk up, sweeping her black bangs out of her eyes, her face taking on a breezy, bracing look. "We could talk about your trip? Tell me things; I've never been there. Did you get offered sex?"

In a way.

I shook my head. "I did not contribute to the sex trade, no. I know you're disappointed; I'm sorry."

Linn huffed through a smile. "You totally did Thailand wrong. Go back."

"Kinda wish I could. It was nice."

"Yeah? Did you take any pictures?"

"Oh, yeah. Um, I was just going through them when you called." Behind the Skype screen I could still see the bottom edge of the photograph of me and Nate; the sides of our feet were touching. I remembered how easy it felt crowding in next to him, our hips mashed together, arms crossing along our backs, his palm curving at my side. Out of view of the webcam, I raised an unthinking finger toward the seam between our shoes.

Linn leaned forward. "Ooh, I wanna see."

My hand flexed back from the screen. "Right now?"

"Yeah. Upload them somewhere where I can see, and then you can give me the lowdown on everything. It'll be like doing vacation slides, only across the Internet."

"Really?" I made a suspicious face into the webcam. "Nobody likes those."

"Pictures, Em," she pleaded.

I capitulated, hands up. "Okay, okay. This'll probably take a few minutes, so tell me what's up with you while I do this."

As she updated me on her adventures in parenting and pregnancy, I navigated to one of my image hosting accounts and started uploading the photos in bulk. On a sudden impulse, I removed the one of Nate from the album; he'd be my secret to keep.

I sent Linn the link, and we went through the pictures together, my dry explanations doing nothing to deter her from oohing and aahing her way through the entire album.

For some reason, though, talking to her about all the people, places and things I'd photographed, however tediously, made them seem more real than before. I had been there, I had done these things, I'd had fun.

"Whoa," she laughed, at an incredibly blurry picture of me, the one where I'd countered Nate's accusation of not smiling properly by then smiling like an escapee of an insane asylum.

Linn clicked to the next photo.

"Oh," she breathed. Her eyes flicked up to the webcam. "Em, who took these?"

In my admitted haste to scroll through all the pictures to get to the one of Nate, I hadn't noticed this one, which appeared to either have been taken by accident or on the sly, just after my unleashing of my maniacal smile. The picture was simply one of me laughing, because, I remembered now, Nate had been laughing.

"You look so happy there," Linn added, a curious lilt in her voice.

"Yeah, um, it was this-- I kinda made a friend when I was down there," I said.

In an instant, Linn went from slightly awed to full-tilt saucy. "Ooh, what kind of friend? Would I approve?"

Would she? Maybe. We'd never find out.

"A friend friend," I said unhelpfully. "A pal. A chum, some might say."

She made a scoffing noise. "I said what kind of friend, not give me useless synonyms for friend."

I rolled my eyes at the webcam, though it was unlikely she'd see it, her attention on the picture album. Still, I did it for the principle of the thing. "It was just-- this guy. We started talking one day and then... we hung out a bit." *And then I slept with him.*

"Is he cute?" she asked.

"Uh," I said, caught off guard. Why would she even ask me that? Did she know something I didn't know she knew? I fell back on a safe, "What?"

"Why is it," Linn said, "that guys always have so much trouble talking about whether other guys are hot? You don't ever see women having this problem. I can tell you five gorgeous women I'd go gay for right now."

She reeled off her list, which I could find no fault with.

"Yup," I agreed. "If I were you, I would also have no problem going gay for them."

She frowned at my circumvention attempt. "Do you have a picture of this guy? I will tell you objectively whether he is cute, and then when this comes up again, you can save yourself all that spluttering."

"Linnea," I said, in my most reasonable voice, "you're the only person I know who would ever ask me if some guy I met on vacation and will never see again is cute."

"Then you need better friends in your life," she said, mimicking my tone.

"You're all the friend I need," I said, overflowing with saccharin. "Hey, how's Clark doing?"

"My dearest hubby is great, thanks for asking," she said brightly. "And if he were party to this conversation, I think he'd agree with me that it's so cute how you're obviously trying to change the subject."

I grimaced minutely at the webcam, really not wanting to get into it. "Most people would be polite enough to let the subject change."

"Excuse me, did you just compare me to most people? You take that back," she said.

"Come over here and make me."

Linn snickered. "Okay, look, I'm not going to pry, even though you know I'm dying to. But if, whenever, you want to talk about it, I'm just a Skype button away."

My irritation melted away. I didn't want to talk about it, but it was nice to have the option. "I know," I said.

She smiled, reassuring even from three thousand miles away. "Good. So, what the hell is up with this thing? Are those tentacles?" she said, moving right along to another picture. "Did you actually eat this? It looks awesome."

We finished up the album and talked a little bit more about inconsequential things, my mind only half on the conversation.

I did actually want to tell somebody about Nate, about how crazy and unexpected it had all been, about how well we had seemed to fit together. But what would be the point? Whatever I was feeling now or might feel in the future didn't matter because I was never going to see him again.

And then there was a part of me that was afraid of voicing any of it at all. Once I hung real words on it, I wouldn't be able to take it back. I liked Nate. Some part of me that wasn't occupied with licking my wounds probably still loved Michelle.

Where did that leave me?

***

The remainder of my weekend was spent first calling my parents to assure them that I was alive, and then scrawling as many thank-you cards as I could get through without wanting to throw my fountain pen out the window. It seemed a bit unfair that on top of being the one left, I also had to be the one relegated to the task of writing things like:

Dear Aunt Patty,

Thank you for coming to be a part of what definitely ranks in the top five worst days of my life. While your generosity is much appreciated, I am returning this gift, as forced bachelorhood necessitates total abstinence from bamboo placemats and matching napkin rings in my daily life.

Sincerely,
Emory

Too much?

Hal came over to pick up the gifts that could be dropped off locally, and did exactly that, saving me the trouble and embarrassment of showing up at my relatives' houses myself. The rest I had to haul over to the post office, single-handedly saving the United States Postal Service from bankruptcy with the shipping costs alone.

That done, Hal came back with a six-pack, and we watched a soccer match on TV for the rest of the evening. Despite us exchanging probably no more than two non-soccer-related words, I felt better for having him around.

We had treaded the sticky waters of middle school together, as unlikely of friends as we had been -- I, scrawny and single-minded in my quest for straight A's, and he, a laidback, gentle giant happy to camp at the peak of the bell curve. We had been paired up one morning for the badminton unit in PE, found each other relatively tolerable and, later that day, he'd come to sit at my lunch table and then just never left. I never asked why he'd decided to sit with me and my similarly gawky, high-waist panted friends that day, but it turned out well for the both of us. He ended up being the only friend I'd keep from those hazy days of pre-algebra, Illinois history and the hot shame of adolescence.

Even after I trotted off to college and he stayed behind to work at his dad's contracting company, we'd managed to stay in touch somehow, though my memories of him are largely unaccompanied by any kind of soundtrack, his presence big enough to make words unnecessary. He'd always been comfortable with silence, knew when to speak and when not.

And now was a time for not. He didn't ask things like, "But how are you doing, *really*?" or do that sympathetic head-tilt at me; he didn't make me talk about my feelings; he just brought me beer and let me sit and eat nachos in peace, and I couldn't have appreciated it more.

Work was a vastly different circumstance on Monday morning.

I left the apartment with steel in my spine, ready to laugh off any mentions of my misfortune, but of course nobody would let me.

"Oh, honey," said Marybeth at reception as soon as she saw me trying to sneak into the clinic without anyone seeing.

"Please don't," I said.

"Okay," she said, a crease appearing on her already well-lined forehead as she peered solicitously at me over her purple-rimmed reading glasses, "but there's a casserole in the fridge for you, and you know, if you need anything else, you let us know, okay, hon?"

I mustered up a smile; even if unneeded, it was still nice that there were people willing to look out for me and occasionally feed me the best of Southern home cooking. "Thanks, Marybeth. I appreciate it," I said, and fled to the sanctuary of my office, where I huddled in the tepid glow of my computer screen until it was time to see my first appointment.

The day went on with other staff and therapists either speed-walking past my office or popping their heads in, well tilted, to give me bucking up speeches. I also somehow managed to amass a large handful of chocolates toward the end of the day, one of which I decided to set aside for my four o'clock client as a choice of reward if she did particularly good work, which was usually the case.

I went out to the reception area to get her. "Hi, Abby," I said, giving a short wave to her and her mother. "Julie."

"Hi, Mithter J," said Abby, smiling the untroubled smile of five-year-olds everywhere.

"You look so tan," said her mother, as we walked farther into the clinic toward my therapy room. "Is that from the honeymoon? How was the wedding?"

"Uh," I said, wondering how to make her stop, though clearly it was my fault for having blabbed about being affianced in our biweekly before- and after-session small talk. "It wasn't."

Julie's eyebrows came together, plainly confused, and I held my clipboard higher in front of my chest to protect myself from what was inevitably to be another pitying look. But then I had already collected so many today; what was one more?

She caught a glimpse of my left hand, holding the clipboard aloft, and noted the distinct lack of ring. "Oh," she said. "Oh my god, I'm sorry. What happened? Oh my god, I'm sorry, again, that is clearly not my business."

"It's okay," I said evenly. "Things just didn't work out."

And there was the look.

"That's a shame," she said. "Anyone would be lucky to have you."

I had been getting quite a lot of that, too. In theory, it was a nice thing to be told, but the obvious underlying assumption there was that I had been the one dumped, which seemed telling, especially coming from people unaware of the circumstances. Was it my face? Was my chin too pointy to warrant even a modicum of happiness? Was there some deeply ingrained, inherent Other Guy-ness about me that rendered me forever to wallow in second fiddle territory?

"Um, thanks," I said, because there was nothing better to say. "Okay, well, I guess we should get started. Come on, Abby, we have a couple of cool new games today."

While Julie stayed behind in the adjacent observation room, I took Abby to our therapy room, and by the end of the session was able to unload the chocolate I had saved for her, which was a pleasant end to a thoroughly awkward day.

By the end of the week, the chocolate dwindled along with the platitudes.

By the end of the month, things were nearly back on track to approaching normalcy. It helped that somebody else in the clinic broke her arm on a weekend ski trip, so she got put on casserole watch instead, and I, thankfully, slipped out of the office consciousness.

It seemed that I slipped out of Michelle's consciousness as well by that time, the number of her calls declining until finally there were no messages left to erase.

Subsequently, her absence from my life became something less of a black void. Occasionally I'd think of her and feel a deep need to go and cry in the shower, or throw something breakable at something even more breakable, but these too passed eventually, until I could think of her and convince myself that I felt almost nothing. Some days I was more convincing than others.

It was harder with Nate, which I hadn't expected. Compared to the years of history I had with Michelle, Nate was, or at least should have been, an insignificant drop in the ocean. But the few days we'd had together were as near to perfect as anyone could reasonably imagine, and with him, there were the tantalizing threads of *what if*.

What if that near perfection could have gone on forever?

What if I had already let go of the best chance of happiness I'd ever had?

What if he was mine? What then?

As much as I knew it was useless to keep following those threads just to see where they led, I couldn't shake the urge off. Even when I was getting better at suppressing them, they would come at me out of the blue; a certain kind of build of a stranger who walked past me on the street, the color of the sky on a particularly sunny day, the aroma of something almost identifiable -- anything and everything seemed capable of looping back to Nate somehow.

I imitated normalcy as best as I could, practicing at it in the hopes that one day it would take, but there were the quiet nights here and there when I'd lie awake, challenging the ceiling to staring contests and asking it what if.

And the more I chased these endless threads, the clearer it became that I couldn't call it an aberrance anymore, couldn't completely ascribe it to being a different me for a week, because a bolder, more intrepid me still housed *me* at his core. It wasn't just that I had enjoyed Nate's company, it was that I had *liked* him, so much and in so many ways, and trying to get the gist of what that meant was bringing up all kinds of unsettling, inarticulate thoughts that I couldn't sift through on my own.

Finally, sick of driving myself crazy, I flashed an emergency distress signal to Linnea. I needed someone else, someone with more credibility than myself, to tell me to get a grip. If I had her in person I could count on her to shake me by the shoulders in addition, but getting her to shout at me over Skype would have to do.

"Hey, hon." She was wearing her glasses, the thick, black-framed ones that meant business, her long hair gathered at the top of her head in some half-hearted approximation of a bun, and I was afraid I had interrupted her working on something more pressing than my existential crisis, but she smiled and said, "What's up?"

I stopped my frantic chewing on my thumb for long enough to say, "I sent you an email."

"Uh, and you called me just to tell me that?" Linn said flatly, though from the video feed I could see that she was already checking her inbox.

I watched her click the email open and could pinpoint the moment she downloaded the file I'd attached, a photograph.

"This is the friend you made in Thailand," she said, not at all a question.

"Yeah," I said.

"Em, what kind of friend?" she asked, though it sounded like she didn't really need me to answer and wanted me to say it for myself, the way teachers patiently extract answers they know you know, somewhere in the jumbled mess of your adolescent mind.

"A we-slept-together kind of friend." There, now it was real, and I couldn't unmake it.

Linn looked at the picture again. "Well, he *is* really cute, so..." She gave me two thumbs up and a questioning grin.

"Did you know? That I'm..." I wasn't sure how to finish the sentence, the words available to me too restrictive and too expansive all at once.

"Kind of, I guess. I suspected," she mused, resting her chin on the heel of one hand. "There was this guy who lived down the hall from me, you know, during grad school, and I so wanted to set you up with him, but then you started dating Dani, and then Michelle after that, and then you almost got *married* to her, and then I thought I probably shouldn't give him your number after all."

"Well, I probably wouldn't have taken it anyway," I said.

Linn frowned. "Why? I have impeccable taste. He was totally cute, and in med school. Dude, you could be dating a doctor right now."

I shook my head, chuckling softly. "I wasn't-- I don't--" I said, unable to find what I wanted to say. Slowly, struggling to get my thoughts in order, I added, hoping she would understand what I was trying to get at, "I wouldn't have let myself."

"Why?" she asked again, softer this time.

It took me a minute to marshal the honesty that the question deserved, to call to mind memories interred somewhere deep down and far away. I had always been a bit different, keenly aware of it, eager to resolve it, but not knowing quite what it was that set me apart from the other boys. I liked all the same things they liked -- Super Nintendo, trading cards, whichever girl was deemed the cutest in our class that year. And whichever boy was cutest in our class, I liked him too. It didn't occur to me not to, though I learned quickly to chalk it up to admiration rather than attraction, and eventually, not to think of it at all once I realized I wasn't supposed to.

"I never do. I never have," I said quietly, half to myself. "It's just easier that way, you know?"

It had been a lot easier, in fact, carrying around a vague sense of dissatisfaction, as most people do, for one thing or another, than shouldering the guilt of being different, and it had been easier, in many ways, to try harder at being not different, until trying became an entrenched habit in itself.

I looked, sometimes, but never let it get any further than that, guilt-ridden enough with that tiny indulgence, knowing intellectually that it wasn't wrong but feeling bone-deep that it was.

Armed and delusional with the false security of being un-Emory for a week, Nate had been the first time I'd ever let myself feel what had always simmered underneath the carefully cemented, fortified, steel-reinforced surface, and now I couldn't not feel it. How unfair that I had built all those defenses with all that work, and Nate could simply come along, tap a little chink in it and make it all crumble away like it was nothing.

It was freeing, in a way, saying these few words to Linn, letting them out of the barbed-wire cage of my head, but mostly it was terrifying. I couldn't take back what I'd said about Nate, and I couldn't take back what I'd said about myself either. I knew she would never let me, and maybe that was why I'd come to her in the first place.

"I just didn't want to be different from all the other kids, and I guess it stuck," I said. "And I still don't want people to look at me now like I'm different."

Linn nodded in understanding but said, "You know the people who matter will just look at you like you're *you*, right? I mean, honey, I'm looking at you right now and you look the same as you did, like, five years ago. It's really infuriating, by the way, how you haven't aged at all, and I know you don't even use moisturizer, so that's doubly enraging."

A laugh bubbled out my throat unexpectedly. "I can't help it if I have good genes, okay?"

"Ugh, so unfair," she said. "But hey, just for the record, there's nothing wrong with a little guy-on-guy action. Many women find it quite hot, in fact."

I laughed again, glad to have called on her services. "So you're saying that if I swing both ways, that actually works in my favor?"

"You'll have to beat them off with a stick, my friend. Especially if you're doing it with this Thailand guy, because he is-- I mean, seriously, well done." She fanned herself.

"All right, we've hit the point of diminishing returns on helpfulness now."

Linn chuckled, and accordingly turned her levity down to a low simmer. "What's his name?" she asked gently.

"Nate. Harris."

"And what brings Nate Harris to our discussion table today?"

I worried the inside of my bottom lip. "I can't stop thinking about him," I admitted in a rush, cringing at how ridiculous I sounded. A few more confessed feelings and I'd have a cloying pop song on my hands.

"How can I help?"

"Tell me to stop?"

"Okay," Linn said. She took a moment to think. "Em, you're just coming off a three-year relationship. It ended horribly, and this guy happened to be there to pick you up. It felt good only because you needed something good."

I nodded vigorously as I listened, as if the harder I nodded the better her words would stick with me.

"And, you know," she went on, losing the sage edge a little, "obviously yay that you learned something exciting and new about who you are, and good job to Nate Harris for bringing that out in you, but you don't need him anymore. You learned what you needed to learn from him, and now it's time to move on. You're rebounding, really hard. But that's all it is."

"Okay," I said.

Linn peered at her screen, trying to read my expression. "Yeah? Was that good? Are you cured?"

"I'll have to get back to you on that," I said.

It helped to have somebody tell me what I already knew, but getting over the idea of perfection that I'd built up in my head wasn't going to happen overnight.

"Fair enough," Linn said. "If you feel the urge to have stupid squishy feelings about him, just slap yourself as I would slap you, if I were able."

"Hm, no. I don't see that happening."

"Okay," she said, shrugging. "Then just make Hal come over and do dumb guy things with you, like watch the football and do kegstands and crush beer cans on your head."

"I'm almost thirty years old, Linn. My bones are getting too brittle for that."

She laughed. "Whatever. Just find some way to distract yourself whenever you can."

"Will do."

"And call me if you relapse," she said, her mom voice creeping in now.

My nose screwed up in disagreement. "What, so you can yell at me for not listening to you?"

Linn gave the question its due consideration. "Yeah," she decided. "Pretty much, yes."

"Bye," I said, and hung up the call after she waved her goodbye.

Renewed in my resolve to forget Nate, or at least to shove the memory of Nate to a dusty and disused corner of my mind, I got up from the computer and went in search of a distraction.

It was too late to call Hal to come over and play, so I was left to my own devices. The fridge produced apple juice and leftovers, and my DVD collection was sufficiently stocked with movies that featured lots of blood being shed and things getting blown up.

Picking one at random, I fed the disc in and eventually fell asleep to the soothing strains of ticking time bombs and rapid gunfire, dreaming of a wonderful life in which all of my problems were just as easily solved.

Chapter Six

My mind settled down once I started shaking my life up.

Taking Linn's directive and giving myself distractions, I rearranged some of the furniture in my apartment, discovered how to use more than one machine at the gym where I'd apparently held membership for the past year, and bought a new gaming system. Granted, they were very small steps, more trembles than shakes, but they were something.

Things were, against all odds, looking up.

Which, of course, is the primo time for life to pitch a curveball right at your head, and I didn't have the wherewithal to duck in time.

More precisely, I didn't have the wherewithal to cheese it out the clinic emergency exit, upon going to the reception area to collect my four o'clock client and finding Nate sitting next to her, threatening a tickle with waggly fingers. She squealed, he laughed and my stomach swan-dived off the nearest cliff.

What was he doing in my clinic? With my five-year-old client, no less, and her mother nowhere in sight? I hadn't heard an Amber Alert on the news. But surely people didn't kidnap children for the sole purpose of bringing them to their speech therapy appointment? That would be madness. And I knew madness intimately.

"Oh my god," I said, "what are you doing here?"

Abby, who appeared in fine health and not particularly perturbed about being abducted by a handsome stranger, hopped off the chair, blonde pigtails bouncing. "Hi, Mithter J."

"Oh, hey, Abby," I said, which was really the first thing I ought to have said and in my normal pitch range. "It's good to see you again."

"Yeah," she said, smiling as she twisted her body left and right.

I got on one knee so I was level with her. "Where, um, where's your mom?" I asked, flicking a glance at Nate, who looked mildly entertained, which was I thought was unreasonably audacious for a kidnapper.

"Work," Abby replied. "Uncle Nate brought me."

"Oh, uncle, ah," I said, seeing the family resemblance between her mother and Nate now that it had been revealed. "Ahh."

Nate rose from his chair, a glimmer of amusement still on his face. "Yeah, Julie had some kind of work emergency, so she asked me to get Abby for her."

"Ahh," I said again, suavely. "Okay. Uh. That's--that's very nice of you. Okay. Well. Are you ready for speech, Abby?"

She nodded brightly and turned toward our regular therapy room. Before I could follow suit, Nate touched my elbow lightly.

"Hey, Mister J?" he said, the corner of his mouth turning up slightly at the sobriquet. "Julie said there's an observation room she usually sits in to watch the session; is it okay if I watch?"

I blinked at him. "Sure!" said the ghost of my prepubescent voice while the rest of me tried to stave off a cardiac episode.

In graduate school we'd been forced to get over whatever self-consciousness we had while conducting therapy, as all our clinic training took place in therapy rooms with two-way mirrors concealing the critical scrutiny of our supervisors making notes on our every move on the other side, to make sure they could later tell us the myriad things we did wrong. To make things even scarier, clients' parents, spouses and caregivers, as well as keen undergrads, often sat in with them, judging our worth as future therapists to be sicced on the general populace.

When not frightened out of our wits, we often felt incomparably silly. Administering therapy for young children usually involves games, toys, storytime with appropriate animal noises, and a hell of a lot of exaggerated surprise and encouragement. *Oh my goodness!* we gasp with delight. *What a good R sound you made there! You are such a hard worker!*

Eventually we learned not to mind the watchful eyes on the other side of the mirror, and if we felt silly, at least we also usually had fun with it.

And maybe it was just time that had softened the corners of my memories, casting a rosy haze over those hundreds of hours of being silently observed, but I couldn't remember a time when I had felt more exposed than I did now, knowing Nate was watching me.

I mean, this was a person who had seen me in excessive states of undress; how could I not feel at least a little foolish?

The feelings settled down to manageable levels as Abby and I sat at the table, studiously and efficiently going through a set of picture flashcards featuring colorful line drawings of short words beginning with S.

Seal, soup, sock, sand.

'Sand' made my cheeks feel warm, on association with a particular nighttime beach situation, but I determinedly did not look in the mirror to survey how obvious of a flush stained them.

We cruised through much of my lesson plan without incident, but then as we wiggled around the room, pretending to be snakes and hissing S-words, I couldn't help but feel like a complete idiot.

And then I felt like a complete idiot who wanted to kick Nate in the shins.

I mean, the unmitigated *gall* of this man to show up at my workplace unannounced, looking for all the world like he's just glided off the runway at Fashion Week, and make my insides twist themselves into a series of sheepshanks and ask politely if he can watch me work. And if that weren't enough, to actually follow through on watching me work and making me feel twenty-two again, beleaguered with doubt and all at sea.

Of course, that was all assuming that he was actually watching and had not wandered off in search of something more exciting than the proper pronunciation of esses. In fact, I quite hoped that he had wandered off.

"All right," I said, giving Abby a high five as our session came to a close. "You did great today. Don't forget to show your mom your notebook so she can help you at home with your snake sounds, okay?"

"Yesss," Abby hissed carefully.

I thumbs-upped my approval. "Nice," I said. "Okay, let's go find Uncle Nate."

Given that the observation room was immediately next door we didn't have far to go. Gingerly, I turned the knob and eased the door open, somewhat surprised to find Nate still in there.

"Ah, hi," I said. "We're all done."

"That was awesome," he said, taking Abby's hand. He grinned at her. "Mister J's pretty cool, huh?"

"Uh huh," Abby agreed.

Nate nodded sagely. "Julie raves about you," he said.

I avoided Nate's eyes and focused somewhere above his left ear. "Um. Just, you know, doing my job. So, there's a notebook in Abby's backpack with a list of words she should practice for next week."

"Got it," said Nate. He nodded seriously at my instructions, and then tossed a lopsided smile at me as Abby, bored, began tugging him out into the hallway. "I may have promised frozen yogurt."

I walked them back out to the reception area. "Okay, see you next week, Abby," I called out, and got a frantic wave in return.

Nate paused at the door, hesitant. "See you around?"

Unlikely. "Yeah, sure. Okay. Bye," I said, meaninglessly, each word more unnecessary than the last.

They continued to the parking lot, out into the summer heat, making funny hissing sounds at each other, from the looks of it, and I stood in the shadow of the door, watching Nate walk out of my life forever. Again. Probably for real this time.

I mean, what are the chances?

***

To: ejames@petersensc.org
From: nathaniel.harris@nmharrisstudio.com
Subject: Hi

Hey, I hope this is okay. I got your email from your business card at the front desk. It was really good to see you last week. I'm going to be in town for a while -- do you want to meet for coffee sometime?

-Nate

***

I reread the email fifteen times before concluding that there was an eighty percent chance that I wasn't hallucinating it, and if the email wasn't an elaborate figment of my imagination, then Nate showing up at my clinic hadn't been either.

Chewing industriously on the side of one thumb, I let my cursor hover over the 'Reply' button.

Did I want to meet for coffee sometime?

It was an easy question, but finding an answer to it was infinitely more complicated. *Hell yes* sprang to mind immediately, but so did *Hell no*.

I'd been doing so well lately with not indulging all my what ifs; they were like children -- sometimes ignoring unwanted behavior makes it stop. They had almost stopped, I thought, but obviously they'd only been quietly regrouping to muster up the means for a last-ditch attempt at shredding my sanity by dropping Nate, solid and real, right in the middle of my path.

And I couldn't decide whether running to him or simply running away was better form.

Opting to concentrate, as best I could, on work for the moment instead, I closed out of my email without sending a response.

Thirty seconds later, I opened it again and typed *Yes*.

Honestly, I'm surprised I lasted that long.

***

A series of short, polite email exchanges landed us at a downtown coffee shop on a Saturday afternoon.

I arrived ten minutes early to scope it out and to be seated when he arrived, in case my knees decided to stop functioning at the sight of him; it had been fairly touch and go when he'd appeared in the clinic, and I didn't want to take any chances with sudden solubility.

He breezed in right on the dot, windswept from the funnels of wind that regularly tore through the maze of downtown architecture, his face lighting up when he caught sight of me seated in the corner. I waved from my table by the window as he walked over, vivid in dark blue stripes, sunglasses perched atop his head, his cheekbones and the slide of his nose rubicund from the warm summer sun, and I quietly congratulated myself for having the foresight to sit down first.

We shook hands, just as we had the first day we'd met, which seemed absurd, given everything that had gone down between us, but I wasn't sure I could handle anything else anyway, or what was actually appropriate to do when getting reacquainted with someone you'd had sex with while on vacation.

Should've Googled it before I left the house.

After we both got our coffees, he asked, "How have you been?"

"Uh, good," I said, though why I bothered lying was anyone's guess. Deserted at my own wedding, falling into bed with a near stranger, rediscovering sentiments I thought I had buried under six feet of cement long ago, said stranger suddenly popping up again out of nowhere -- I wasn't good, I was flummoxed.

"Yeah, well," Nate said, smiling softly. "You look good."

"That's probably because I realized one day I was getting direct debited for a gym I didn't even remember signing up for and went to recoup my losses. It's always nice not giving away money for free," I rambled.

He smiled some more. "Looks like it's working out really nicely for you."

"Um," I said, feeling my face get warm. I fiddled with the handle of my oversized coffee mug and tried for normal conversation that didn't involve me. "How long did you say you're in town for?"

"Uh, a while," Nate hedged. He rubbed the back of his neck, an abashed move, and glanced at me from under his lashes. "I just moved here last month."

I'm not sure what kind of utterance I had intended on making, maybe something unflappably urbane like *Why, that's wonderful news! We simply must get together for cocktails once you're settled in.* But even the best intentions had no chance at stifling what essentially emerged from my throat as a tight gurgle.

It was not a sound I looked forward to making again in polite company, but I could hardly be blamed for my lack of composure. I mean, I had only just come to terms with what my life was, with the fact that there was a Nate somewhere out there in the world leaving swoons in his whirlwind wake, and that world wasn't mine.

And then I had, with what I thought considerable sangfroid, accepted that the strange whims of the Nate somewhere out in the world were just flitting him, by the law of probabilities, temporarily past my path again.

I wasn't prepared, however, to deal with the Nate somewhere out in the world whose somewhere was permanently here.

Nate gave me an anxious glance. "Look, I'm not stalking you or anything, I promise. I didn't even know you lived here until I had to bring Abby to your clinic the other day."

"Right, yes," I said, nodding even though I was too ill-equipped to properly suppress my bewilderment.

"And then when I found out she was seeing you -- I mean, I had hoped it was you, because how many Emory James speech therapists can there be?"

I shook my head, confounded by the question, among other things. "I don't know, I could check?" I said, ludicrous and wheeling off in some distant universe where this wasn't actually happening.

"I really didn't think I'd ever see you again. But then there you were. And I said to myself, 'Self,'" Nate said, the restiveness on his face giving way to something softer as he tentatively held my gaze, "'if you don't invite him out for coffee you'll regret it forever.' So I did."

The rules of conversation, curse whoever invented them, required that I respond in some fashion, though what that fashion was I had no clue.

"I'm glad you did," I said, surprising myself. To prevent the conversation taking a mawkish turn, I barreled on with a jaunty, "So, if not to stalk me, then what made you decide to move here?"

"Well, with the divorce and all, Julie's got her hands really full, so I thought I'd come and help out, especially since I can make my own schedule. I've been wanting a change for a while anyway; I wasn't that happy in San Francisco."

Oh, San Francisco, that's where he was from. Cross that off the checklist.

"You guys are close, huh?"

He nodded, smiling. "She gets me. She, uh..." he said, trailing off with a little reticence in his voice, not entirely sure he wanted to say what he'd been about to say. He looked at me for a moment, deciding. "I came out to my parents when I was sixteen. They were pretty... not okay with it, but Julie was always on my side. She got me through a tough time. So now it's my turn to get her through."

It was a hard fight not to reach out and touch him then, to ease some of the tightness out of his shoulders.

Coming out to your parents. What was that like? Not a barrel of monkeys, I'd imagine.

"So, yeah," Nate said, rallying. "Here I am."

"You liking it here so far?" I asked.

"Yeah, yeah, it's cool. I really like my neighborhood; it's up north a bit, in Edgewater, and I'm pretty close to the lake," he said, "right on Granville and Kenmore."

I stared into the placid surface of my black coffee, and my gently undulating reflection showed me a face fixed in incredulity. "I live four blocks from there," I said.

Was this fate? If so, fate really needed to tone it down a notch or four thousand.

Nate's eyebrows knitted together. "Are you serious?"

"Yeah," I said. "This is weird."

Nate agreed. "I guess maybe we're destined to be friends, huh?"

It wouldn't be the most terrible thing in the world. Take away the hot sex, and he was still someone whose company I enjoyed, assuming the Nate I had met on vacation was the same Nate whose real world had just collided with mine. I wouldn't judge; I had been a different Emory down there, too.

Well, I'd probably judge a little.

"I think I'd be okay with that," I said after a while.

"Cool," Nate said, and we shared a little grin of understanding.

We were starting over, starting at the point we would have before, had we been normal people who'd met under normal circumstances. Being friends would be fine; it'd be great. And if that turned into something different as we went along, well, I'd panic at that bridge when I came to it.

We talked about him moving his business up here, and about places around our neighborhood that were recommended and not, all wide, open spaces of impersonal dialogue we could just as easily have had with someone we'd never met before. It was odd doing this with him. We'd pretty much skipped this part before; it felt like I had checked out the ending of a book first to see if I liked it before starting on Chapter One -- which some people consider cheating, going straight to the end first, but sometimes it's nice knowing in which general direction you're headed. There are so few circumstances that even allow it.

"So, um," Nate said, after a brief lull in our conversation, one finger describing the smooth, ceramic rim of his mug. "Mind if I ask about your fiancée?"

Okay, I guess we were officially moving out of brand new friend territory, and toward the infield of privileged information. I couldn't decide if he was being nosy, presumptuous or merely concerned. I suppose, in all fairness, I *had* brought it up at one point, a very inopportune point, at that, and had just left it to loom.

"Ex-fiancée," I cleared up, shrugging as though it was water off my back. "Left, like I said, on our wedding day. Hasn't come back."

She had returned the engagement ring -- my Grandma Violet's -- before taking off to parts unknown with Good-Looking Bastard, pressing it into my hand with promises that someday there would come along someone better suited to wear it, which pretty much sealed the *ex* part.

Nate made a small, sympathetic noise.

I frowned. "I can see that you're about to tilt your head at me and say something uplifting, so if we could not go there, that would be excellent."

"Sorry," he said, nodding his agreement. "I'm sure you've heard all the empty platitudes in existence by now."

"And more," I said, doing a half-hearted impression of a TV announcer.

"Do you miss her?" he asked. His mouth pulled downward suddenly, and he hastened to add, "Sorry, that was a really dumb question, and very much not my business."

It really wasn't, but there's something to be said about telling your business to someone with no stake in it. It's why occasionally it's easier to open up to a stranger than to someone who knows you. There's less judgment, less useless, if well-meaning, advice, less expectation.

Nate wasn't exactly a stranger, but he didn't exactly know me either, here in my natural habitat.

"I'm getting better at not missing her, if that counts," I said.

His eyebrows rose, surprised that I had picked up his question. "It does," he said.

Though he asked nothing more of me, I apparently had more to say that I hadn't been able to say to anyone else. My problems had long since ceased to be disclosable to my parents; released into the wilds of college and beyond since eighteen, smart enough to vote but still too dumb to be allowed alcohol, the difficulties encountered thereafter were officially mine alone. Hal and I, bound by the inexplicable rules of manhood, communicated in ways that occasionally suggested that post-Paleolithic evolution had never happened, and Linnea had always made it clear that she thought I could do better.

With the people closest to me out of the running, what I had left was the man sitting opposite me, someone who didn't really know me and knew even less of Michelle, and that in itself made it easier somehow to loose my thoughts on him.

"She was really easy to like, you know?" I mused. "She's just one of those people."

Nate nodded. "How did you meet?"

"I did my clinical fellowship at this nursing and rehab center over on the West Side, and she was-- still is-- Well, I don't know anymore, maybe she isn't," I said.

Who knew what she and Good-Looking Bastard were up to in their wild, unfathomable existences? He was from New York, that much I knew, as most Good-Looking Bastards seem to be; maybe she was scattering the ashes of our relationship into the Hudson River as I spoke, while he looked on from the prow of his massive bastard yacht.

"At *some* point, she was a nurse there," I said. "I met her on my first day on the job, and we shared a couple of patients, and she was always so bright and kind and... Not especially good at forward planning, though, considering what happened."

"What did happen?" Hurriedly, Nate added, "If it's okay to ask."

My mouth screwed to one side, my bottom lip catching in between my teeth. I suppose it was my own fault for not cutting off his line of questioning earlier, and now I could add another name to the laundry list of people who would see me for what I was -- deficient.

"Her ex-boyfriend crashed our wedding, which apparently in some cultures is a socially acceptable romantic gesture," I said.

"Bastard," Nate interjected.

Involuntarily, I laughed, his conclusion so very similar to the ongoing narrative I had in my head of their exploits. "I concur," I said. "But she didn't, obviously, and they took off to parts unknown. I have absolutely no idea where they are; down the street, for all I know. God, I hope not, though."

Nate, peering out the storefront window, shrugged an ambivalent shoulder. "Could be. I see a dude who looks like a meth addict across the street; I'm going to assume that's what this fiancée thief looked like, right? I mean, obviously, the only reason she would have left you for anyone else is if she suddenly lost her mind and got struck blind on top of it. Pretty action-packed, your wedding day."

I looked at him askance. "I don't think that's quite her version of events."

"Yeah, well," said Nate, "she's not here, so I'm just going to have to go with my version."

"I could buy into that," I said, after a moment's consideration.

"Excellent," he said, grinning. "Then you're going to love next week's installment in which he develops spontaneous alopecia."

I laughed again, his absurd scenarios making me feel so much better than all the empty words of comfort that had been shied at me ever since the wedding that never happened. "I can't wait," I said.

I hadn't said all that I could have said, like the first inkling I'd had that Michelle might be someone more special than most when she carelessly, brilliantly threw a Tom Servo quote at me; like how she had been the one to ask me out on my last day at the rehab center, just before I took my current job at Dr. Petersen's practice; like how needlessly nerve-wracking the proposal had been because her father accidentally told her about it beforehand.

They were memories for a book I needed to close. Besides, Good-Looking Bastard was a meth addict now and about to lose all his hair, and that seemed a satisfactory enough end to that particular story.

I take my victories where I can.

Chapter Seven

Exchanging cell phone numbers turned out to be something of a mistake, if only because Nate's indiscriminate text messages over the next couple of months, often informing me of random though interesting facts about his day (*Abby given access to J's old lipstick and my face. Send help!*), created a Pavlovian reflex in me, a little skitter of happiness that ran through me whenever my phone trilled with a new text.

There was no point denying to myself that I was still attracted to him, though I kept that route closed off with a dozen rolls of mental caution tape. Whether he felt the same I didn't know, but neither of us broached the subject, happy enough with the status quo of occasionally getting together for lunch or coffee and idle chatter.

"Hey," he said one day over the phone when I picked up with a feeling more of curiosity than anything since his communication method of choice was usually texting and I hadn't yet been conditioned to perk up at the sound of incoming calls.

"Hi, what's up?"

"I want you to say hi to somebody special," he said, bubbling over with ebullience. His voice became distant as he talked to someone in the background. "Hey, come here. Come say hi to Emory, babe."

My heart sank before I could save it, and then buoyed back up again out of morbid curiosity when I heard some shuffling and then a bark. "Uh, Nate?" I said, not sure whom I was addressing on the other end of the line.

"I got a dog!" Nate announced.

"Congratulations," I said, somewhat breathlessly, feeling my heart swim back to its moorings.

"I think this will make it at least thirty percent more likely that people will come and talk to me on the street when I'm out walking her," he said. "No one can resist the face of a Lhasa Apso; it's been scientifically proven."

I laughed. "You got a dog so people would talk to you? That's really sad, man."

"Nah, that's only the side benefit. Chicago's awesome just as she is. Aren't you, Chicago?" he said, eliciting another happy, faraway bark.

It took me a minute. "You named the dog--"

"After my favorite musical, yes. Well, not my absolute favorite, but it would be cruel to name a dog Les Miserables, right?" he wittered, but I could hear a big, wide smile in his voice that told me the truth.

I smiled into my chest. "I'm sure the two of you will be very happy together," I said, not entirely sure whether or not I was actually speaking in code.

"One can only hope," he said.

We hung up, and I stood with my cell phone pressed against my chest for a moment, where hope and caution were starting a slapfight with each other.

What were we doing? There was always an element of flirtation in our interactions, just because that was the best way we knew how to operate with each other, but this was something on an entirely different level.

Maybe we weren't so happy with the status quo after all.

***

After deciding that the surprise dog announcement had gone over with me well enough to keep calling, Nate called again a few nights later, this time because he was bored.

I glanced at my bedside clock as I picked up the phone and turned down the volume on my TV, while the weatherman gestured to cartoony icons of sunbursts all over the state, just as he had almost every day for the past month, in an unusually dry summer.

"How did you know I'd even be awake?" I asked suspiciously.

"Because you're an informed and responsible citizen who watches the news every night," he replied, and damn him, he was right.

"Well, I never claimed to lead an exciting life," I sighed, as a truck commercial rolled by.

"I never said you needed to," he said diplomatically. Abruptly switching subjects, he added, "Do you think it's weird that after we kept running into each other in Thailand and then here, we haven't at all these past couple of months even though you live four blocks from here?"

I made a face at him, though it lost most of its effectiveness over the phone. "Did you call just to ask why we never see each other even though we saw each other last weekend?"

"No," he said. "I called to ask if you wanted to come with me and Chicago to the dog park on Saturday."

"Oh, I was supposed to get that from all that rambling?"

"Excuse me, Harrises don't ramble; we hold enlightened discourse."

"Oh, is that what you call what happened last week when you spent ten minutes telling me about the new Canadian bills after I asked if you had change for a twenty?"

A chuckle tumbled through the line, the familiar sound of it immediately bringing up an image of the way his eyes crinkled whenever he laughed. "Yeah," he said, "and don't you feel more enlightened now?"

I slid an inch down the headboard, switching the TV off now that there was no more news to be had. "I feel sleepy now."

"Do you need a bedtime story?"

"Yeah, tell me more about Canadian currency."

Nate laughed again. "Fuck off. I'll text you about Saturday."

"Okay," I said through a yawn. "Night."

Setting my phone back onto the nightstand, I turned off the light and shimmied further down the bed, pulling the bed covers up. My mind replayed our conversation, and though there was nothing particularly interesting or informative in it, I couldn't help but smile into the darkness.

***

Somehow, the switch from exclusively texting to actually speaking to each other over the phone opened a kind of gateway for us, and instead of the occasional coffee of simple acquaintances, we began making the kind of plans friends do, long, sunny days of casual meanderings across a windy city in which I had lived for years.

That seniority made me the default captain of our wanderings, something of a reversal of the us in Thailand when Nate had been happy to sport the imaginary tricorn and I content to tag along. It was nice being able to share the little things I liked about what I suppose could now be considered my hometown with someone else; the skyscrapers and museums were great for passing through, from what I'd heard, but it was the small, inconspicuous places, I thought, that glimmered like little pieces of its soul.

I brought him to my favorite bar, where they didn't try to deafen you with the Top 40 and had a shelf of board games you could play with for hours; let him in on the secret of a fantastic little Cuban restaurant tucked away in the back of an unassuming Rogers Park grocery store; introduced him to a beer garden with the best burgers in the Upper Midwest a few short blocks from where we both lived.

It was something I had never quite done with Michelle, who'd always preferred the artsy glamour that the city exuded with equal aplomb.

Not, obviously, that I had anything against the arts, and decided one day, realizing with a bit of a start that summer would soon be coming to an end, that Nate needed to experience the season closer of the Grant Park Music Festival.

"Hey," I said, calling him from my office phone, "you free tonight?"

"It's Friday night; sadly, of course it means I'm free."

"Do you have any kind of blanket you won't mind getting dirty?"

Nate was quiet for a moment. "Why?" he asked. "Do you have a corpse you need to dispose of or something? Oh my god, who did you kill?"

"Really? I ask if you have an extra blanket and that's where your mind goes? I'm seriously starting to reconsider this friendship."

He tutted. "I think the point you're missing is that I was willing to come and help you dump a body into the lake. If that isn't the mark of a good friend, I don't know what is. A little appreciation would be nice, man."

"Let me rephrase," I said. "Do you have a blanket you wouldn't mind getting *grass stains* on?"

"Yes," he said primly.

"Okay, bring it. Meet me at Michigan and Washington at six, right by the park?"

"Done," he agreed. "What are we doing?"

It hadn't occurred to me, several months ago, occupied with trying to remember how to breathe after Michelle had left, that I had missed the spontaneity of being on my own -- doing, eating, seeing whatever I wanted without having to check in with anyone, making plans on the fly, answering to myself alone. And it was nice that there was somebody else as unencumbered as I was to be spontaneous with me.

"Just bring the blanket. See you at six," I said, settling the receiver back in its cradle before Nate could ask more questions.

With that taken care of, I slipped out of my desk chair to go and get a client file from the cabinets in the clinic's front office.

As I thumbed through the files in the R section, I became increasingly aware of Marybeth eyeing me sideways. I removed the file I wanted, sticking an orange out card in its place, and closed the file drawer carefully; as it snicked into place, Marybeth pivoted in her chair to face me directly.

"Why are you smiling like that?" she asked suspiciously. "You've been smiling like that for weeks."

I froze, my hand still on the drawer handle, as though I'd been caught doing something unseemly. "Like what?"

Marybeth frowned, not really sure herself, and went with, "Like you have some kind of juicy secret you're not telling me."

"Well, that is the nature of a secret, not telling people," I explained, which was exactly the wrong thing to say, though I'm not sure that denying the existence of a secret would have made much of a difference.

"What is it?" she demanded, the chain of her reading glasses swinging pendulously as she leaned forward, an expectant glint in her eye.

"Nothing," I said. "There's no secret. I'm not even smiling. You know I don't smile; I am stern and unyielding."

Marybeth narrowed her eyes at me, my litany of refutations obviously falling on deaf ears. "Okay," she said airily. "Keep your secrets if you must."

"I shall," I said, removing my grip from the filing cabinet and heading back out into the hallway behind her. "If I had any to keep."

"Mmhm," she said flatly.

Whether it was the power of suggestion or whether her eyes really hadn't deceived her, I began noticing too that my face was occasionally going rogue the rest of the afternoon, smiling when I had little reason to smile. Maybe my facial nerves were developing a neurological condition; I resolved to keep a close eye on it.

When the work day finally came to a close, I packed up quickly and said hurried goodbyes to anyone I happened to pass by on my way out, including Marybeth, whose best wishes for a nice weekend came with the bonus gift of another one of her oblique glances.

I squeezed onto one of the Red Line trains, shoulder to shoulder with all the other commuters eager to leave work behind, and it spat me out at the Monroe stop, where I popped into a nearby deli to pick up a couple of sandwiches and drinks to go. A couple of blocks north, I found Nate waiting, a dark green fleece blanket rolled up under one arm and the white string of a pair of earbuds disappearing into his back pocket.

He extracted the earbuds on my approach, smiling. "Where's the body?"

"You're a very disturbed young man," I said. Jerking my head toward the deeper recesses of the park, I added, "We're going this way."

Once he realized where we were headed, his grin widened. "Cool," he approved. "I've been meaning to come all summer."

We unrolled and flapped the blanket out onto a patch of the expanse of lawn that yawned around the open-air, silver-shell stage of the Pritzker Pavilion; chairs and music stands for the orchestra were already set up, patiently waiting for their players. It was still early, and there was a steady stream of people arriving and staking out their spots on the green. A couple of small children tottered past us, squealing as they chased one another through the warren of picnic blankets and lawn chairs.

"I didn't even think of it till now; tomorrow's the last performance for the season," I said.

"Well, at least we get today," Nate said, kicking off his shoes and settling himself onto the blanket, lying on propped elbows.

Comfortable on the fleece, we stared up at the sky for a moment, the exact shade of cornflower blue you get in back-to-school crayon packs and dotted with tiny wisps of clouds that scudded by on invisible currents. We couldn't have asked for better weather for a free outdoor concert.

The wind made the plastic bag at my side rustle, and I remembered that I had brought dinner. Rooting for our sandwiches, I found Nate's first and handed it over. "Roast beef," I said. "I told them no onions, extra tomato. Correct?"

"A-plus," Nate said, a note of surprise in his voice.

I tilted my head in acknowledgement. "I am amazing."

"That you are," he said, and tipped the soda bottle I passed to him in cheers. He cranked the cap off and took a swig of it, looking around at the rapidly filling up lawn. "Man, I'm really glad I have you to do all this stuff with. I mean, I have Jules and Abby, but that all has to be kid-friendly, you know? Not that this isn't, but."

I nodded, carefully unwrapping my pastrami on rye. "Yeah, I get what you mean."

"It's hard to meet people, you know? Well," he amended, "not hard to meet them; it's hard to keep them."

"Everyone's already got their own things going on," I said.

"Yeah," Nate agreed. "And there's work, but then there are only three people who work at my studio, including me. There's, y'know, Rita, who does all my bookkeeping, and then my assistant Valerie -- you met her that one time."

"Yes," I said, remembering being confronted with very blonde, very bright, youthful exuberance when I'd stopped by Nate's studio once, a modest street-front office space he rented slightly north of downtown.

"Rita's sixty, and she spends her days off with her husband and cats and diverticular disease," he went on. I gave him a perturbed look, and he appended, "She tells me these things; I can't make her stop. Besides, she's a superstar at accounting, so if she needs to tell me about the degree to which she feels bloated on any given day, I'll take it."

I chuckled. "That's very big of you. But yes, I can see why the two of you might not socialize well outside of work, though."

"Yeah, and then of course Valerie's, like, ten. Fresh out of college, so she goes and does whatever it is the nation's youth do for fun these days."

"Drink?" I suggested. "Breakdance? Use the Twitter?"

Nate patted me solicitously on one shoulder. "Well, at least I'm not as old and out of touch as you."

"Only by a few months, my delusional friend," I pointed out, returning the gesture, a little harder. "I look forward to the day when you're as cranky and confused as I am. What a great day that will be."

"No," he said. "I refuse."

I clicked my tongue at him. "Okay, Ponce de Leon."

He laughed. "Ponce de Leon? Wow."

"See, that's one of the benefits of being friends with me. You get a higher class of reference," I said. "You thought I might go with Peter Pan, or even one of your Botoxed celebrities, but no, you get sixteenth-century apocrypha."

"Impressive," he conceded. "And still so old."

We finished our sandwiches contentedly, watching the people around us settle in. A young couple spread a blanket a few feet in front of us, the male half of whom was one of those unfortunate souls afflicted with the disorder that convinces them the world needs nothing more than an all-access view to their underpants.

"That's unseasonal," I said, of the young gentleman's candy cane boxers. They were red and green on dingy white.

"Stop staring," Nate laughed.

"It invites judgment," I sniffed. "Are belts so difficult to manipulate? It's a *loop*."

Nate lay back, framing his supine head with crossed arms, and closed his eyes, half a smile on his face. "Simmer down, grandpa."

I thwacked him lightly on the arm. "That is no way to speak to your elders."

He reached up and yanked me down onto my back as well. "There," he said, pleased with himself, "now you don't have to look at his ugly underwear anymore."

"That's no way to treat your elders either," I said, though I made no move to lever myself up again, comfortable where I was. I was vaguely aware that lying down after eating may occasionally result in heartburn but decided not to mention it; the wisps of cloud that waved to us from above were too pleasant to spoil with talk of esophageal reflux. Plus, I didn't want Nate to never speak to me again.

Eventually, the performers began to stream onto the stage to smatterings of applause from the people who had opted for the plastic chairs immediately in front of the stage rather than sprawling on the lawn like the rest of us common folk.

Over the next hour, we let the music weave its threads around us, telling haunting stories of love and loss. When the story was over, applause thundered over the lawn, and Nate opened his eyes and smiled, his skin burnished with the light of the setting sun. Its burnt orange rays stained the stage shell's curves and boughs in its likeness, and it reminded me of a past life, when Nate and I had watched the sunset together. A cool lake breeze blew in, and if not for the lack of sea salt in the air, I might have easily imagined we were back in that life long gone. I let the thought go on a gentle coil of wind.

The orchestra exited the stage, giving way to a low hum of a hundred conversations starting up at once -- *where did we park again; wasn't that fantastic; Mommy, I gotta go potty* -- though Nate and I added nothing consequential to the rabble, merely turning toward each other with the shared smile of a shared experience.

We waited out the crowds as they picked up their belongings, all headed toward the restrooms or parking garage or back to the street, where they would travel in large herds on the L until handful by handful they fell away to wherever the night intended to take them.

When the crowd had dispersed to less of a bovine situation, Nate and I picked up our garbage and rolled up the blanket. He tucked it underneath his arm, and we walked together back to the train station, lucky to have a train come rolling in after less than a minute's wait.

Against the rumbling clack of the train speeding through the underground, it was quiet in the car, most of the passengers intent on showing off the latest in handheld devices. Neither of us broke the silence, content to simply sit side by side, contemplating the subterranean dark and then the low-rise facades that whizzed by once we made it out of the tunnels.

At Argyle, the train lurched a little more violently than usual, knocking our knees together, and when it carried on chugging along, neither of us moved away from the contact. It didn't mean anything -- at least, it most likely didn't, but I was aware of the light thrum of nervousness underneath my skin anyway, a staticky sort of energy building restlessly on itself, like it was waiting for something to move, waiting for something to change, though nothing did.

My stop came first, and I swung around the handrail, breaking the tenuous bridge between our bodies, and waited for the doors to ease open. "Night," I said to Nate.

He smiled, enigmatic. "See you around, Chicago."

***

After that, there were movies, a Cubs vs. Astros game and another concert, an African fusion thing, featuring a kora player he kind of knew from San Francisco. We cycled through every single meal of the day, even the portmanteau ones, I taking him to the hidden gems I hoped the mainstream crowd never discovered, he taking me to places that proved exactly why they'd earned the adoration of the mainstream crowd.

Autumn blew in on a cool, golden breeze, painting the town red and yellow. We swapped out short sleeves for long, missing nary a beat in our exploits, some meticulously planned and others cobbled together in a capricious minute. When icicles started decorating the city's eaves, we added scarves and jackets to the mix and continued on, bumping shoulders as we forged furrows in the snow on our way to the next great thing.

They weren't always supremely exciting, these next great things; we revisited several places multiple times -- the beer garden, for example, housed a roaring fireplace inside during the cold months and still served the best burgers money could buy -- well on our way to earning regular status. What made the next great things great was simply that we were doing them together, that we were finding such ease and understanding in each other's company.

I had, by this time, succumbed to classical conditioning with my ringtone as well, involuntarily smiling to myself whenever my cell phone shrilled, involuntarily smiling even more when it lit up with Nate's picture, always happy to hear him tell me what we were going to do on any given day, even if it was just to grab a quick lunch together in the middle of the work week. I didn't ask, though I wondered if he was as behaviorally modifiable as I was, but he seemed equally happy when the shoe was on the other foot, whenever I was the one to ring him up and ask him to gallivant somewhere with me.

It could be that I was imagining it, or projecting something of my own onto him that wasn't there, but I couldn't, or didn't want to, make that explanation stick. Something in his voice, an indecipherable timbre of fondness, when he spoke with me seemed absent with anyone else; something in his face, a subtle softness in the curve of his smile, seemed reserved only for me. And I knew I wasn't imagining the way I was around him, brimming with tightly lidded affection, meticulous about never letting it spill, but never happier than when we got to spend hours doing anything or nothing together.

How dangerous exactly was this game we were playing?

We flirted, madly, with each other and with the careless expectation that anything could happen again, even though we never let it.

Before, it had been something of a moot point, as there was a professional code of ethics that wouldn't have allowed anything between us anyway. But I had discharged Abby several months ago -- her esses were smooth as silk now, not to toot my own horn -- so, really, the only thing now standing between me and Nate was, presumably, me and Nate.

We could never erase what had arisen between us in Thailand, not that I wanted to, but did that mean we were obliged forever to carefully, quietly sidestep our past every time we so much as looked at each other?

We never talked about it, so how long would it be before the elephant trampled everything in the room and knocked all four walls down?

"It's kind of like we're dating," I explained to Linn and her six-month-old, whose apple cheeks and jet-black hair were exactly like her mother's but who, unlike her mother, was deeply indifferent to my maunderings, "without getting to, you know, make out and stuff."

Linn frowned at her screen. "That's a bad place to be in," she said. "Well, what do *you* want out of it?"

"I don't know. We spend all this time together, constantly, and... and I don't know."

What I couldn't articulate was that there was always an undercurrent of something more between us, something tempting and terrifying at the same time. We were moths circling around a flame, a warm, gold flicker that kept daring us to come a little bit closer. How close could we get without getting burnt?

"I like him," I said, and paused to roll my eyes at myself for the term I was about to grudgingly employ, a term I thought I had long ago banished from my brain, along with all other memories of junior high, "and I *like* like him."

In my defense, like liking someone makes you stupid. It's not my fault.

"You could pass him a note later in Biology, asking if he likes you and to check yes, no or maybe," Linn said dryly.

"Shut up and tell me what to do."

"Honey," she sighed. "As much as I would love to be your puppet master, I can't decide these things for you."

I furrowed my brow.

"Okay, you're making a confused face at me now. What is this face?" she said, her hands gesturing an arc at the screen.

"I don't know if it's worth it. I mean, he's great, and he's a great friend."

"And you don't want to risk ruining the friendship," Linn finished.

I nodded, my shoulders sagging. "And even if we did start... something, what if it all goes horribly wrong? And then if we broke up, I wouldn't have him in my life at all. So maybe it's just better if we stuck to whatever this is now and left it as it is?"

"Maybe," Linn said. "But you're also kind of forgetting that there's an equal chance of it all going right."

"So what do I do?"

Linn let out a sympathetic chuckle. "Again, you really need to stop tempting me with absolute power over your life."

"Decide. Decide for me," I said, tired of running the same scenarios over in my head, tired of calculating my odds and coming up empty each time. "I grant you power of attorney."

"In that case, this is what you're going to do," she said. "You're going to stop sitting around and asking yourself what if while the rest of the world passes you by. You're going to do what your heart wants you to do."

"Yeah, but what if my heart is wrong?"

Linn clucked her tongue in reproval. "What did I just say about not asking what if questions anymore? Were you even listening? I just dropped a giant pearl of wisdom back there."

I made the same noise at her. "I'm serious. It's been wrong before. You do remember Michelle, right? It was hideously wrong that time."

"No," Linn said firmly. She shook her head to punctuate the point. "You weren't wrong, Em. She was."

My eyes narrowed in the suspicion that Linnea was just talking nonsense now.

"Besides," she continued blithely, "you would've never met Nate if Michelle hadn't been a raging asshole, right? At the risk of using up all the world's cliches in one conversation, sometimes things happen for a reason."

"Things happen," I agreed.

"Follow your heart," she commanded, pointing an imperious finger at me.

"Well, okay," I said reluctantly, "but if this ends badly, it's definitely going to be your fault."

"I'm a mom, Emory. I'm never wrong."

***

Following your heart is, I daresay, a lot easier when your head doesn't interfere with its endless chatter of doomsday scenarios, each one more devastating than the last, full of hearts shattered beyond repair and friendships irrevocably sundered and, once, a factory explosion.

(That one was the full-length, action film version.)

Presumably wherever Nate and I ended up, if we moved at all, wouldn't involve plastic explosives, but the possibility of a ravaged relationship in the end still loomed large and real in my mind.

Of course, this was all only half of the equation. As hopelessly chaotic as my thoughts were, constantly scuffling for dominance in my head, at least I knew what they were.

Nate's thoughts were less transparent to me, though he did call in the early evening, a few days after Christmas, to say:

"Emory, did you know you're my favorite person in the world?"

"I did, in fact," I said, sticking a finger in between the pages of the book I'd been trying to finish while the clinic was closed for the holidays. "I'm assuming it's because I'm about to agree to help you with something I don't really want to do?"

"And so astute."

Fifteen minutes later, I stood under the black awning at the entrance of Nate's red brick apartment building, an overnight bag hanging from my hand.

It had occurred to me, earlier on the phone with him, that he could have kenneled Chicago rather than getting me to dog-sit, but -- cards on the table here -- I didn't mention the option to him because I'd never seen his apartment before. I was curious. It was one of those things we were careful about while being heedless with everything else; inviting a friend back to your apartment takes on a vastly different connotation when you've slept with that friend, no matter how long ago it was, no matter how much time you've spent together since then determinedly not sleeping with each other.

I buzzed, and the front entrance unlocked with a light snick.

Carpeted stairs drank in the melted snow from my footsteps as I walked up to the second floor and found Nate's apartment unit with the door ajar. The door swung open then, revealing Nate in its frame with his cell phone pressed to his ear. He beamed at me and motioned for me to come in.

"Yeah, no, no, it's totally okay, Jules. It's not your fault. Anyway, it's all taken care of; Chicago's in good hands," he said to his phone, and mouthed a *Sorry* to me.

I waved it off, taking in my surroundings, awash in neutral, minimalist tones. I wasn't sure if that meant Nate simply lived an uncluttered kind of life, or if he wasn't planning on putting down many roots here.

Chicago pattered over to me with a raggedy chew toy in her mouth. "Hi, dog," I said, leaning down to scratch her behind one ear.

"Yup, okay. Love you too," Nate said, and hung up the phone, slipping it into his back pocket. "Sorry. That was Julie. They're still stuck in Detroit; the weather's pretty bad out there, and I guess none of the planes are going to get out today."

"Oh, man, that's awful. The Detroit airport's the worst place to be stuck in," I said, giving Chicago one last pat before straightening up. "Hey, how come you didn't go with her and Abby to your parents' for Christmas?"

Nate's hands, which had been fiddling with a low stack of file folders on his coffee table, stilled abruptly.

"Oh," he said, not quite looking in my direction, "my folks aren't exactly eager to see me."

It was the kind of statement that invited a whole host of other questions, but I wasn't sure whether it was my place to ask them.

He resumed neatening the stack and tucked them into the laptop bag at his side. "Um," he said after a moment, his mouth twisting to one side, "I told you I came out to them when I was sixteen, right?"

"Yeah," I said slowly, and already I could tell I wouldn't like where this story was going.

Nate nodded. "Yeah, well, they kinda kicked me out a little bit after that when they realized it wasn't just a phase. I haven't been back since," he said, shrugging in resignation.

"Oh. God. I'm sorry," I said.

"Well, what can you do?" Nate said, the lightness in his voice anything but genuine. He manufactured a bracing smile from thin air. "Okay, uh, dog food's in the pantry, and you're welcome to whatever's in the fridge, or anywhere else. So, make yourself at home."

"Okay."

"Thanks for doing this for me, man. Especially on such short notice."

"Yeah, of course. No problem," I said. "Just think of it as you owing me a favor."

Nate laughed, and I was glad to see his heart in it this time.

"Big time," he said, patting me on the shoulder as he passed toward the open kitchen. He stuck his head in the pantry and emerged cradling a six-pack of energy drinks. "Almost forgot these babies."

I stood watch, hands in my pockets, while he double-checked all the photography equipment he was taking with him on this job. "I still don't understand why anyone would have a midnight wedding ceremony."

He shrugged, unperturbed by the concept. "They think it's romantic. And they said they wanted to dance till the sun came up."

"It's the middle of winter. The sunrise is going to be bright gray."

"Hey, as long as they pay me, I don't care what kind of wedding they have," Nate mused. He picked up the multitude of bags containing his equipment and lifted his car keys off a hook next to the door. "Okay, I'll see you tomorrow. Have fun. Bye, Chicago!"

"Drive safe," I called down the corridor as he left, and shut the door behind him.

The evening passed uneventfully; I made a sandwich while Chicago crunched on her dry dog food, and we watched a few sitcom reruns together. Afterward, I fell asleep on Nate's couch, the pillow and blankets he'd set out for me carrying the faint scent of his laundry detergent.

Somewhere out in the suburbs a wedding party soft-shoed to the sunrise, while I remained in bed -- in sofa, rather -- until the morning news was over, after which I took Chicago on a walk through the neighborhood. The sky was overcast and the winter air chilly, but she didn't seem to mind, toddling along and stopping to smell what I could only infer were thoroughly thrilling odors every few yards. A couple of joggers passed us by, bestowing adoring smiles on Chicago's irresistible little face. They glanced at me fleetingly, but my face didn't warrant similar adulation, which was patently unfair, as, between the two of us, I wasn't the one who bathed only twice a month.

When we returned to the apartment, Nate still hadn't. Expecting him soon, I unclipped Chicago from her leash, coiling it around my fist and hanging it up, and set to folding the spare blankets and repacking my overnight bag. Chicago whined at me, padded a few steps away, and then looked at me expectantly. I took a curious step toward her.

"How can I help you?" I asked.

When she rinsed and repeated, I got the feeling I was supposed to follow her.

"I swear to god, if Timmy's fallen down the well again..." I said, and followed her lead toward what I deduced was Nate's bedroom, the door to which was shut. "Uh, I don't think I'm allowed in there. Let's just leave Timmy to his fate; I mean, he has to learn sometime, right?"

She did not appear to appreciate my heavily outdated wit, pawing insistently at the door.

"Fine, you go get him. I'll stand guard out here," I said, opening the door with my back to the room to let the privacy of Nate's bedroom remain private.

I heard Chicago whuff at something, her nails scrabbling against the hardwood floors. She padded back to the door, whining at me again.

"This is a fun game," I said dryly. "Look, if no one's dying in there, you're just going to have to leave it until Nate comes back."

Chicago gave me a long, mournful look and then sneezed on my foot.

"That seems a disproportionate response."

I started to close the door, but she darted back into the room, so I decided to leave the door ajar until she came back out again. When she started barking, however, I had no choice but to at least poke my head in to see what she was kicking up such a fuss about.

Next to an unmade bed, Chicago danced around Nate's nightstand, occasionally trying to squeeze her face into the few inches of space between its underside and the floor.

Since privacy protocols were already breached, I walked into the room and got on my hands and knees to see whatever she was trying so hard to get at. Underneath the nightstand, resting casually against the wall, I could see the shadowed outline of a small rubber ball.

"Seriously? You couldn't wait another thirty minutes for this?"

She whined.

I reached under, my fingers closing around the ball. It squeaked, and Chicago, in her happy haste to get at her resurrected toy, pushed at my arm as I was pulling it back out. She jarred it hard enough that the nightstand tottered, and a precarious stack of paperbacks made a break for the floor, scattering.

"There," I said, tossing the ball back out to the living room. "If you lose interest in it within the next ten seconds after all that work, there will be words."

She bounded after it, and I was left to clean up the mess. Along with the books there were a couple of photographs on the floor that may have been used as bookmarks, and as I picked them up, I couldn't help but notice the familiar face featured in them -- mine.

There was the one of us together -- I remembered Nate asking that lady to take the picture on his camera as well as mine, and another of me in profile, one that I hadn't even been aware had been taken at the time, framed by the same expanse of sea and sky as in the first photo.

After a moment of mute staring, with only the sound of my heart to accompany me, I arranged the books and pictures carefully on the nightstand, and exited the room, pulling the door shut.

Chicago was cheerfully squeaking her ball along the plush floor rug in the living room. I sank onto the sofa and watched her gnaw at it for a while.

"Well," I said, "I guess that little excursion turned out to be quite fruitful for the both of us."

At that moment, I heard a key slide into the front lock, and turned to see Nate walk in, a bright smile on his face, despite having been working the whole night.

"Hey, guys," he said, setting his bags down. "How did it go?"

"Uh, good," I said awkwardly, as I got up from the sofa and moved toward him.

Nate glanced down at himself and then back at me, the beginnings of a perplexed frown on his face. "Are you okay?"

"Yeah, why?"

"You're just looking at me really weird," he said, getting on his haunches to pet Chicago, who had been trotting around his ankles in greeting.

I thought of the photos at his bedside, could easily imagine him taking them out at night to ask himself what if. Maybe I was wrong, but maybe I wasn't. We had been dancing around each other for so long now;

maybe it was time to change the steps. Maybe it was time to let my heart take the lead.

"Hey," I said, shooting for casual and landing somewhere near awkward teen. "How much would it ruin our friendship if I kissed you right now?"

Nate rose, staring at me while Chicago padded off somewhere else.

"I don't know," he said slowly, taking a step toward me. "How much do you want to find out?"

Quite a lot, as it turned out.

I surged forward, my hand curling around the back of his neck, pulling him to me. The space between us vanished in an instant, taking uncertainty along with it as we collided, lips and hands remapping long-lost territory.

There was a thrill of newness and the comfort of familiarity all at once; the tautening of his muscle cords underneath my fleeting fingers, the lush heat of his breath on my lips, the echo of our pulses as they raced each other, they were all things I remembered and learned again.

His hands skimmed a trail along my back, searing his touch into my skin, and I couldn't remember the last time I had ever wanted anybody this much.

***

"Not that I'm complaining," Nate said some time later, his fingers idly climbing up and down the ridges of my collarbone as we lay in his bed, "but what brought this on?"

"Let me preface this story by saying that Chicago made me do it," I said.

I explained Chicago's insistence at getting into his room and at her ball, and finished the story by plucking the photos from his nightstand and handing them to Nate.

He smiled softly on receiving them and murmured, "Good dog."

"But seriously," I said, "I'm sorry about coming in here without your permission. I wasn't trying to snoop through your stuff or anything."

Nate dismissed the apology with a shake of his head and a light kiss to my shoulder. "I don't care, man; it's really not a big deal. Anyway, I'd say it worked out in both our favors, wouldn't you?"

"Pretty much, yeah," I agreed. I looked at the photos in his hand. "When did you take this one?"

He chuckled. "That was by accident. Remember I was showing that woman how to use my camera? She accidentally pressed the shutter release. It turned out a surprisingly good photo, though."

"Yeah, I don't look like a serial killer at all; it's weird."

"You're weird," he announced mildly, prodding a sleepy finger into the side of my face.

"And you're falling asleep," I said, sitting up and peeling the bedcovers away. "I'll leave you to it; you had a long night."

Nate's hand landed on my arm. "Wait, come here," he said, and raised himself up on one elbow to meet me halfway for a lingering kiss. A drowsy smile curved his lips as he pulled away and fell back onto the mattress. "Okay, now you can go away."

"Idiot," I said fondly, giving his shoulder a light shove, and tipped myself out of the bed.

Our clothes were in a haphazard mess on the floor, along with the scattered remnants of our friendship, and I picked my way through them carefully, pulling on my boxers and T-shirt on my way out the room.

After shutting the door quietly, I landed on the sofa again, grinning to myself and unable to stop.

Chicago sauntered past, the little rubber ball clamped loosely in one side of her mouth, and gave me a sideways, knowing look.

"Well played, dog," I said. "Well played."

Chapter Eight

Although I would have liked to stay forever, and Nate did his level best to keep me tethered to the bed with whispered entreaties that made my insides dissolve to liquid heat, I was due at my parents' for New Year's weekend, in lieu of my annual Christmas visit.

They had booked a cruise along the Floridian coast long ago with the understanding that Michelle and I would spend our first married Christmas together with her family. And just as I had refused to let my honeymoon go to waste, whether or not I had a wife to come with me, I'd refused to let my parents cancel their plans either.

Nate, come to see me off, wrapped his scarf around me, folding a deep red knot loosely at the hollow of my throat. "It's cold," he said, patting his handiwork. "And now you'll have something to remember me by."

"They live a two-hour drive away, and I'll be gone for a weekend."

"Hey, man, it's this or a lock of my hair."

I gave him an oblique glance. "You're weird," I said.

Nate grinned. "I know, and you're the one who likes me, so who really comes out on top here?" he said, echoing a similar, carefree sentiment I'd tossed at him way back in Thailand.

It felt like so long ago, a different life ago, and made our current relationship seem even more surreal.

"I can't believe you're using my own words against me."

"We can fight about it when you get back, and then make up in all kinds of super fun ways," Nate suggested, his voice dipping to a husky register I was starting to recognize as dangerous.

Falling right into it, I kissed him, and forgot to stop, and that was how I ended up at my parents' house an hour later than I had initially planned.

I parked in the driveway and dug my keys out of my bag to let myself in.

A wall of central heating enveloped me as soon as I stepped into the house, along with it the smell of old wood and the echoes of my childhood.

The house had been around for a long while, its bones and furnishings a tribute to the decade when my parents had first moved in with a chubby-fisted toddler in tow. There were a handful of newer things, too, a flat-screen TV, a sleeker dishwasher to replace the one that had died and leaked its remains all over the linoleum, but for the most part the house remained as I had grown up in it -- flowery pastels, dark wood furniture, geometrically patterned mirrors; it was practically a time capsule in itself.

Unbidden, a picture of me bringing Nate here flashed across my mind, Nate with his skinny jeans and artfully tousled hair and big city charm, and he looked as incongruous here as the flat-screen did, out of time and out of place.

But that hadn't stopped my parents insinuating the TV into their home either, so maybe he'd be dissonant but not unwelcome.

I shook my head of the thought, feeling absurd and oddly guilty that I was considering it at all. It hadn't been that long ago when I'd dragged Michelle here, nervous, unutterably nervous that the most important people in my life would discover that the only thing they had in common was being tied to me.

They had liked her well enough, Dad more than Mom, but civility wasn't the same as warmth.

It had occurred to me then that my only child status might have had something to do with it, the inability to cut the apron strings and all, or possibly because Michelle was staunchly Protestant, and they were naturally suspicious of anyone who swung that way. But then again, maybe they'd known something then that I didn't. People seemed to know a lot of things I didn't.

Setting my bag down and removing my coat along with Nate's scarf, I hooked them onto the coat rack by the door and called a hello to the house, ducking uneasily under the view of the crucifix hanging in the front hall. It was its occupant's job to weigh my worth, after all, and I tried to avoid his eye.

"Emory, honey, is that you?" Mom's voice floated from somewhere upstairs.

We found each other on the landing of the stairs and hugged; it was more or less perfunctory on my part, though at one point in my life, before sullen adolescence had hit, I'd known how to do it wholeheartedly. And now it had been so long since I'd been that boy that I wasn't sure I remembered how, though I sometimes wished I could.

Mom seemed not to mind, holding me for a second longer than usual, the light, floral scent of her favorite perfume as much of a memory marker as the house was, of skinned knees and comfort, of kisses goodnight. We hadn't seen each other since the wedding; ostensibly, this was to make up for any lack of hugging then, when I'd been so blunted that a hug and a punch might have felt identical.

"How was Christmas in Florida?" I asked, getting it in before she could ask, in not so many words, if my heart was still broken.

I wouldn't have known what to say anyway. Being with Nate was keeping the pieces together; that didn't necessarily mean it wasn't broken anymore.

Eventually, Dad appeared too, apparently experimenting with a salt-and-pepper beard now, obscuring the sharp chin and dimples I'd inherited, and we gathered in the living room to exchange the gifts meant to have been given several days ago and to sit through pictures of their trip, reminiscing about things I hadn't been a part of, people I hadn't talked to, places I'd never seen.

To make up for it, they let me talk about Thailand and prompted me to show them whatever photos I had on my laptop. Simply clicking through the entire contents of the pictures folder on my hard drive and doing the same dull spiel I'd done with Linn, I froze for a split second when the picture of me and Nate appeared.

"Oh," I said, "this was a guy I sort of made friends with down there, um, Nate. And funny enough, I ran into him again recently, out of the blue. Turns out he lives really close by, actually. So, uh, we've been hanging out a bit."

Mom nodded, smiling with a slight blankness at my rush of explanations.

"It gets me out of the house," I finished lamely.

Whether all that was me laying the brickwork for a future, more important conversation, or whether I was deliberately downplaying its significance to avoid the same such conversation, I couldn't tell.

Hurriedly, I clicked through the rest of the album, feeling my face burn. I hadn't lied, so why did it feel like I had?

When that was mercifully over, Dad and I whiled away the rest of the afternoon watching a football game on TV in his basement den, beers in our hands; it wasn't something we'd ever done regularly in years past, and it felt strange now, partaking of this quintessentially male-bonding activity when I couldn't feel further away.

I knew he wanted to ask about Michelle, ask how I was coping, ask where my life was now that it had derailed, but he wouldn't, at least not outright. We weren't the kind of family who talked about the things most important to us, so careful to keep our dirty laundry to ourselves that eventually nothing got aired at all.

And even if he did find the wherewithal to ask, I wouldn't be able to tell him everything. I would only say I was fine and leave it at that, because how do you even begin to tell your parents how you have failed, utterly, when not so long ago you had been so sure of yourself?

And how do you begin to tell your parents about something new springing up from the ruins, when the dust from the collapse hasn't even had a chance to fully settle?

So instead we watched the game, making the appropriate noises, drinking our beers, reaching out in our silence and getting silence in return.

We played our mutually unsatisfying game until Mom called us up to dinner.

Over chicken and potatoes, I learned of all the small town gossip I'd missed, living so far out of its sphere of influence. The dissolution of my almost-marriage had probably been going around the neighborhood for a while now, but Mom was careful not to mention what people thought of me now. It was all probably quite deliciously horrible.

Instead, I heard of Tanya from next door getting cheated by the used car salesman on her pickup truck, the row of houses going up with amazing alacrity a few streets away, and of Brian Carter, remember him, he was a senior when you were a sophomore, he was on the basketball team?

I said I vaguely recalled such a person, and Mom, satisfied enough, went on to inform me that he had recently adopted a baby.

"With another man," she said, in a near whisper, as though saying it too loudly might bring the authorities down on us.

"Oh," I said, absently poking at my potatoes. "Good for him."

She gave me a mildly censorious look. "Well, I don't know about that," she said, shaking a head of loose, graying curls. "It just doesn't seem right. I mean, what is the poor baby going to do without a mother?"

I put my fork down. "Hey, do you remember this girl I went to school with called Annie Hyland?" I tried to keep my tone conversational, but it narrowed to an edge anyway. "She was in my class in middle school. She got forcibly removed from her parents' care when she was thirteen, because her mom was on crack," I said, placing extra special emphasis on Mrs. Hyland's drug of choice.

"My goodness," Mom said, a hand to where her pearls would be if she had a string on; her fingers found a delicate gold cross instead. "And her father?"

"Her dad was a dealer," I said, bitterly relishing the look on my mother's face, with silent apologies to Annie Hyland for using her horrible childhood as a parable on stereotyping.

Last I heard, Annie was happily married and had gotten a cushy job as an instructor at an East Coast prep school, so I didn't feel too terrible about it in the end.

"Yeah, so," I continued with dogged blitheness, "I'm not really sure having the proper male-to-female ratio naturally constitutes good parenting."

"How come I don't remember hearing about this?" Mom said, totally missing the point. She touched my father's arm in concern. "Do you remember hearing about this?"

Dad shrugged, shook his head no.

"Oh, Emory," Mom said, "if we had known about all the drugs, we would've put you in a different school. We had no idea St. Innocent's was so poorly managed."

"Okay. Well, thanks, Mom," I said, sagging back into pushing my potatoes around.

Well, what had I expected? No one was going to change their minds about gay adoption just because a girl named Annie Hyland had crappy parents whose only great accomplishment in life had been to shove the appropriate body parts together and spit out a baby who would go on to beat the odds.

And how could I even consider the possibility of bringing up my personal stake in the issue now, when I knew where my parents stood?

I couldn't even find the means to talk to them about the girl who had stamped on my heart with her four-inch wedding heels; how was I supposed to talk about the guy who was helping me nurse it back to life?

The conversation went on without regard to my inner thoughts, winding to other people with other problems, and I did my best to be interested in them.

Mom showed me to the guest room in the basement after dinner, as my old bedroom upstairs, which had been slowly shedding my personality anyway ever since I had moved out, had been converted to a sewing room over the past year. It was a room I wouldn't have needed, because the guest room was the one with the bed big enough for two.

It was just as well, because the stairs going down didn't have the same creak in them as the ones that headed to the second floor, and nobody heard me creep to the front door in the middle of the night to retrieve Nate's scarf.

I fully recognized how bathetic it was, twining the scarf around my fist as I lay in bed, like a lovesick teenager, but it was the one familiar thing I had in a house that no longer belonged to me but to my memories alone.

And how much truer would that be in the years to come?

I thought of Nate and the half a lifetime of estrangement he and his parents insisted on perpetrating. I didn't know what his parents were like, save for that part. Maybe they were like mine, solid, hardworking, wanting the best they could wring out of life for their child, and sometimes just missing the mark.

And maybe my parents were just like them. How much did I want to find out?

At the moment, not at all. Being abandoned once this year had already been difficult enough; I didn't want to make it a habit.

Helpfully, nothing remotely related to the subject came up for the rest of my short stay, and if my parents noticed more distance from me than usual they said nothing about it, not that I would have even expected them to.

It wasn't a conscious move, my increased disengagement, though I suspected it had begun once the discussion on Brian Carter ended, like it would be easier to deal with if I was the one to choose to set myself apart from them, rather than the other way around. They couldn't reject me if I rejected them first.

Some part of me knew I was being petty and unreasonable, that this preemptive strike, however small, was borne almost entirely of self-induced anxiety. Like Linnea had said, I was asking myself too many what if questions and neglecting to recognize that just as everything might go wrong, there was an equal chance that it would all turn out perfectly fine.

I wasn't giving my parents a chance to show me what they were capable of because I knew they were capable of so much. I just didn't know what they would do with it once I asked it of them, and I hadn't the courage to ask.

What if they didn't choose me?

Driving home the following day with this imbroglio building and seething within me, I ended up outside Nate's apartment instead of mine. I sat in the car for a while, the engine idling, staring out the window to his building across the street, its mute facade refusing to relinquish the answers I needed.

My umbrage took a detour, focusing its sights on Nate.

Who was he to come into my life and turn it so far upside down that gravity didn't even know which way to work anymore?

Who was he to make me question the entirety of how I had lived my life before him?

The accusations piled on until I snapped the ignition off and marched across the street and up to the second story of his building, knocking urgently on his door, not even knowing if he was in.

The door opened, exuding warm yellow light from within. "Hey," Nate said, a smile on his lips. "You're home."

Who was he to make me think that this might all be worth it?

"I am," I said.

I kissed him fiercely then, pinning him to the wall, undoing his belt, in an act of defiance my parents would never see.

Chapter Nine

By some divine intercession, if some fans were to be believed, our football team traipsed their way to the Super Bowl that winter. Although I normally retained only a passing interest in the sport, the championship fervor that had overtaken our city and Hal's mind persuaded me to throw a Super Bowl party, in the mistaken belief that it might be fun.

Having invited Hal, obviously, and a few people I was friendly with at work, it took me another few days to decide to ask Nate to come as well. It would've been weird not to, given that he now occasionally spent a few consecutive nights at my place, and I at his, but I was always a little wary of mixing social circles, besides which nobody knew we were even involved.

There were moments when I was fiercely proud that Nate was mine, but only to myself. We had been together for a good month now, and I hadn't told anyone, save Linnea, and then only because keeping secrets from her was an exercise in futility.

For reasons I couldn't properly articulate, I hadn't been able to bring myself to broach the subject with Hal, probably some of the same reasons I hadn't done it with my parents either.

Fear of recrimination, fear of him seeing me differently and not liking what he saw, fear of what that might mean for our friendship? I didn't know, and the more time that passed with my inexplicable reluctance getting in the way, the more I felt as though I couldn't bring it up at all.

Hal came over early on Sunday with a couple of extra chairs and to help out with whatever preparations needed to be done, though that mostly involved him being glued to the pregame analyses on TV.

In the meantime I puttered around the kitchen looking for things that could masquerade as serving platters and starting on a batch of guacamole.

There are few talents I have to boast of, but making guacamole happens to be one of them. I know, it's a gift.

With half an avocado in one hand, I hacked the base edge of a large knife into the seed and twisted to pit it, but my hand slipped, and the blade slid down my palm instead. Instantly, a bright line of blood appeared across the heel of my hand.

"Shit," I cursed. The avocado half in my hand splatted onto the chopping board.

Hal came into the kitchen on hearing me swear, his face blanching a little when he saw me holding a bloody hand underneath the kitchen faucet. "Jesus," he said. "You have any first aid stuff?"

"Yeah, in my bathroom. Check the right drawer," I called over my shoulder as he hurried into my bedroom toward the en suite.

Removing my hand from the water, I gingerly dabbed at the wound with a paper towel, holding it up high so the blood would flow in reverse of the cut. It actually wasn't that bad; the cut wasn't very deep at all.

Hal came back with a tube of antiseptic ointment and a couple of large adhesive bandages, and hovered nearby in stoic concern while I dressed the wound.

"Okay, that looks good," I said, inspecting my hand from several angles to make sure the bandage's sticky edges had been well placed.

"I guess that means no guac?" Hal said.

I arched an eyebrow at him. "You still have two functioning hands, buddy."

"I was kinda hoping you wouldn't notice," he said, sighing, even as he picked up the abandoned avocado and scooped the meat out of it.

Under my strict tutelage, the guacamole managed to come together, just in time for the first knock at the door.

Almost everyone else turned up in quick succession after that, hands full of beer and assortments of heart-unhealthy victuals. With each new arrival, I began to grow more anxious about having invited Nate. What if nobody liked him? What if they did? What if they asked *questions*? I wasn't prepared for questions.

A few minutes after kick-off, Nate arrived, fashionably late and the last of the lot. I opened the door, and out of habit he leaned in for a quick kiss hello, but I panicked and shied away, casting a stealthy glance at the other guests huddled in the living room, who weren't paying any attention to the latecomer anyway.

"Hey, you made it!" I said, several shades too brightly in an attempt to make up for my slight.

Nate saw right through me, however, a small frown forming between his eyebrows. He blinked it away and held up a six-pack, amber bottles clinking softly. "I brought beer," he said, sounding a little wary.

"Great!" I said, still operating on a thousand watts too many.

Familiar enough by now with my apartment, Nate took the beers to the kitchen to stick them in the fridge, and I followed him anxiously, offering my bottle opening services when he removed one from the carrier for himself.

He spied my bandaged palm, a crease marring his forehead in concern. "Hey," he said, lifting my wrist gently, "what happened to your hand?"

Hal walked in at that moment, saying something about chips, and I yanked my hand out of Nate's grasp.

"Nothing," I muttered quickly. "Just a cut."

On sighting Nate, Hal set his chip problem aside and stretched a friendly hand out to him. "Hey, I'm Hal. Don't think we've met before."

Nate shook it. "Nate. Nice to meet you."

"Yeah, you too," Hal said. "So you work at the speech clinic too?"

"Uh, no," Nate said, casting a quick, dubious glance my way. "I'm a photographer."

"He's the uncle of one of my former clients," I interjected, stupidly.

"Cool," Hal said, in his typically taciturn fashion. "Em, where are the chips?"

As I directed him to the top shelf of the pantry, I could practically feel the ire that had clouded over Nate's face come at me in tsunami-grade waves. It was a wonder I managed to remain on my feet at all.

Maybe inviting him hadn't been such a good idea. Maybe not telling one of my best friends about his existence had been an even worse idea.

Keeping up hosting appearances, I ushered Nate out to the living room to meet the rest of the party. He did his part to play the perfect guest and happy football fan, and did it exceedingly well, but I suspected it would take more than a few touchdowns and finger foods to win his good humor back.

The game itself did nothing to help the situation along, as our team, having mysteriously lost the favor of the football gods, received a sound drubbing as early as the first quarter and never won the advantage back.

As the game wore on, my suspicions were confirmed. Although outwardly Nate seemed to enjoy himself just as much as the others did, cheering when cheering was warranted, groaning at bad calls, striking up friendly conversations with the rest of the guys when the clock was stopped, his irritation with me was palpable.

The others seemed not to notice it, but then they hadn't spent months obsessing over him like I had. I noticed it all. It was in the set of his shoulders, in the ripped label of the beer bottle in his hands, in the shifting of his jaw, and I spent most of the game wondering how to make it go away.

At the same time, I couldn't help my own budding irritation with Nate for being annoyed with me in the first place. We'd been together for only a month; it wasn't like I was going to take out a double-page spread in the Tribune to wax lyrical about it. I still didn't know where it was going, or if there was a somewhere it could even go.

The party wound down somewhat early, thanks to our team's dismal performance. One by one, my guests drifted out into the night, nursing varying degrees of grief at our collective loss, leaving only Hal and Nate by the time we officially lost the game by more than twenty points.

I had a feeling Nate was staying only out of spite, like if he stuck around long enough I'd finally admit that he existed in my life in a capacity greater than 'uncle of former client'.

Hal made a half-hearted offer to help me clean up, but I waved him off, sending him home with some of the leftover beer and unopened snacks. He seemed glad to go; I wasn't sure if it was because he sensed the tension between me and Nate, or if he was just looking forward to getting back home to drown his football sorrows in peace.

As soon as I shut the door behind his retreating back, I turned to Nate with my hands up in preemptive surrender. "Okay, I'm sorry," I said.

Nate stood a few feet away, his arms folded across his chest. "For what?" he said levelly, the light of a challenge in his eyes.

I must have been hoping that he'd just accept the apology and we'd be done with it, because the question took me by surprise.

"Um," I said.

"Look, it's not a trick question," he said, sounding tired, as though he'd had this conversation before, "and I'm not trying to pull some passive-aggressive bullshit on you. I know you know I'm mad."

"Yeah. I'm sorry," I said again, and Nate waited while I gathered my thoughts. It took me a minute to find the words for them. "I-- You and Hal are both important to me, and uh, you know where Hal stands in my life, but I told him nothing about you. That was unfair of me, diminishing your importance by omission."

As stilted as it was, I meant it, and the admission seemed to leach some of the irritation out of him, his shoulders relaxing a little.

"But why are you keeping it from him, from everyone?" Nate asked. "I mean, are you-- Are you ashamed of me, or...?"

"No," I said at once, astounded that the thought had even crossed his mind. "Oh my god, no. Jesus, Nate, you're one of the most incredible people I've ever met."

He gave a minute tilt of his head as if to indicate his agreement, and we both laughed a little, easing some of the strain from the room.

I took a couple of steps toward him. "Look, this is kinda hard for me, you know? It's all really... new. I mean, before you, I never even really considered the possibility of being with another guy."

"Yeah?"

"Yeah," I said. "And, you know, I'm almost thirty. Figuring this out now at this point in my life? It takes a bit of getting used to."

Nate nodded, though I didn't expect him to fully understand. He'd found his bravery nearly fifteen years ago; I still wasn't sure if I had any to find. It was one thing to admit it to myself, and another entirely to show everybody else a part of me I had kept hidden for so long. Once it was unearthed, there was no putting it back.

"I just need some time to work it out with myself first," I continued. "But it's definitely not you; you're great. Seriously."

"Okay," he said, reaching an arm out to me. He was sounding more like himself now, a playful confidence coloring his tone as his hand landed on my shoulder. "But just so you know, saying any variation of 'it's not you, it's me' kind of makes it sound like you're trying to break up with someone."

I leaned into him. "You'd think I would've figured that out by now considering how many times it's been said to me."

"They were right, though, all those times," Nate said. "Because who would willingly give you up, unless they had severe mental problems of their own?"

I laughed. "Well, if that isn't the sweetest thing anyone's ever said to me."

"I'm serious," Nate said, his fingers playing with the curls behind my ear. "You, my friend, are a heartbreaker."

"That's not-- No," I said, bemused. "Are you sure you're not confusing me with you? Because you're the one with the tallness and handsome face and a wardrobe not carried over from ten years ago."

"Nope, not confused," he said. He pinched my cheek and I flapped his hand away. "You're going to break my heart someday and you won't even realize it."

He said it so lightly that it could have only been a joke, but something in his face, something focused but fleeting, made me think he actually believed it.

"Well," I said, for lack of anything better to say, "that day is not today."

Nate smiled. He picked up my injured hand, tracing the outline of the bandage with a curious finger, now that he could do it without me freaking out again. "What did happen here?"

I lifted one shoulder to indicate that it wasn't worth mentioning, but then added, "I was just trying to pit an avocado. The knife slipped."

He shook his head. "Man, those avocados will *kill* you. I did the same thing once, sliced my thumb open," he said, showing me a light, thin scar along the length of its pad. "Blood everywhere. I had to get six stitches."

"Oh, are we one-upping each other on injuries now?"

"What? I'm just saying it hurt like a bitch, man. Six stitches!" he said, cradling his hand close to his chest as if the wound was fresh. "That damn avocado; I've never forgiven it."

"Aw," I said, doing my worst impression of a babying voice. "Poor little Nate. Does he need Emory to kiss it better?"

Nate stuck his hand out. "Yes, please."

On impulse, I sucked one of his fingers into my mouth instead, greatly enjoying the look on his face as I slowly released it.

Accepting the challenge, he leaned in close, his breath warm on my ear, his lips barely brushing my skin. "You know," he said, his voice the silk of melted chocolate, "since you're just wantonly dispensing treatment for old wounds, I think I should tell you about this one time when I fell on my dick, so..."

I burst into laughter, shoving his shoulder. "Fuck off," I laughed.

He matched my grin, and pulled me to him again. We came together, tasting the smiles on each other's lips, wrapped in the joy of the moment, in the joy of being us.

And later on, for the sake of thoroughness, I applied my medical expertise to his old injury, and in the end, we agreed that he would probably need repeated treatments. You can never be too careful about these things.

***

Afforded the leeway of taking my time to come to terms with what our relationship meant in the context of the entirety of my life, my procrastination skills kicked into high gear, and I spent the next two months avoiding the topic at all costs.

Nate occasionally talked around it, occasionally asked after Hal and other friends, dropping hints in the hopes of getting in return something better than the ambiguity I kept giving him. But they never quite went anywhere; he seemed wary of pushing me, in case I pushed too hard back.

I knew he was getting a little impatient with me for it, though. Hell, I would get impatient with me, too, especially considering how much time he had let me simmer with it, considering how accommodating and supportive he was being.

Although I recognized -- and quite guiltily, I might add -- that I was taking advantage of his goodwill, I still couldn't actually bring myself to do anything about it, crippled in the fear of losing everyone I cared about in the process.

I was safe where I was, here in my neat, compartmentalized cubbyhole, small and safe, out of sight and out of judgment. I had gone so long, worked so hard at being not different that letting that go felt like walking too many miles in someone else's shoes; those belonged to an Emory who wasn't so afraid of being wrong, of being a disappointment. I couldn't imagine being him. There were so many things to fear, and I feared all of them.

A very sensible part of me knew I couldn't segregate all these aspects of my life forever, but there was also a much bigger, much less rational part of me that insisted that it was all fine, that somehow these hideous complications would work out on their own if I just sat back and let things take their course.

And the longer I let things lie, the worse an idea it seemed to bring them up after all that time, especially given how time seemed to accrue compounded interest in addition. It was admitting to everyone that I had been keeping the truth from them for x amount of time, the x being whenever it was that I had even come to acknowledge that wanting Nate was something very real, and $x + 1$ every intentional day after that.

I was now on approximately $x + 90$, and with each day that passed and with each additional number telling me how many days I had been lying, raising the subject seemed almost an insurmountable task.

And that wasn't even counting the number of days ago that Nate and I had first met and fallen into bed together. That would be almost four times as long a period, and four times as unfathomable a truth to tell.

I wouldn't just be Emory: Now Involved with a Man anymore, I would be Emory: Now Involved with a Man Plus Bonus Web of Deceit. Pull his string, and he'll lie right to your face.

To be perfectly fair, I hadn't out-and-out lied to anyone yet, mostly because nobody had thought to ask yet; omission wasn't quite the same thing, but the distinction wasn't one that most courts would rule acceptable, and I suspected neither would my family and friends.

"You know what you're doing?" Linn said one weekend, obviously well in possession of the answer and so ready to hit me with it.

"What?" I said anyway.

"You're acting like you're just waiting for the end."

"... of days?" I hazarded. "Okay, just because I have an emergency preparedness kit in the back of my closet--"

Linn cut me off with an impatient hand gesture. "You know I'm not talking about the inevitable zombie apocalypse, okay? And wielding a packet of water purification tablets is not going to deter anyone from eating your brains."

"Hey," I said, "you survive our imminent dystopia in your way; I'll do it in mine. With clean, potable water. You can build all the munitions arsenals you want, but they're not going to do anything for you if you're dehydrated."

"Well, I guess we'll see who gets to rebuild civilization in the end," she sniffed, clearly banking on a limitless supply of sawed-off shotguns to carry her through.

I nodded wisely. "I plan to run on a platform of more stringent gun control laws."

Linn narrowed her eyes at the screen. "I think we've gotten off track. What was I talking about before?"

I was loath to remind her.

"Oh, right," she said, and frowned at me. "You distracted me with your post-apocalyptic nonsense. Stricter gun control, my ass."

I lifted my hands, having nothing to do with it. "You were the one who brought up the end being nigh."

"Stop it," Linn said. "You can't weasel out of this forever."

"But I really want to. Doesn't that count for anything?"

"No," she said firmly. "And you can't just sit and wait for someone else to take the burden from you. It's all yours, and you have to deal with it."

I sighed heavily. I knew she was right, and it was maddening.

"Okay, think about it this way. What if Nate just up and left right now? Never came back. What would you do?"

"File a missing persons report after the requisite waiting period?" I guessed, not sure where Linn was going with this.

Her head dropped out of frame, and I heard a muffled groan. When she popped back up, her face filled with vexation, she said, "I'm trying to ask how you feel about him. If the heartbreak of him walking out of your life forever is going to be easier to deal with than what you're going through right now, then let him walk."

"I don't--" I said, having absolutely nothing to follow it up with.

"Okay," Linn continued, taking my speechlessness as an encouraging sign. "Well, then, if you don't want him to walk out of your life forever, you have to sack up and deal with this. He's a great guy, Em, but he's not going to wait around forever."

"You don't know that," I countered lamely.

"Really? You want to test my theory?" Her voice was soft, and her eyes concerned. "Look, you know I don't care who you're in a relationship with as long as they're good to you. Nate is good to you; I mean, you should see your face whenever you talk about him. If he makes you happy, and I know he does, then I'm happy. Have faith in everyone else to tell you the same. They will."

I shook my head, besieged with doubt. "You don't know that either."

"Em, if you lose someone over this, they weren't worth keeping anyway."

"That's really easy to say, but..." I bit the inside of my lip, wondering how to put words to the vertiginous, indefinable clutter of fears in my mind. "Did I tell you Nate hasn't spoken to his parents since high school? They threw him out, Linn, when he came out to them. It's not that easy."

Linn took in a long breath. "Okay, first of all, fuck them. And second, they're not your parents, and they're not representative of any other parent in the world."

"There's a chance that they might be," I said stubbornly.

"Yeah, well, there's a chance you might win the lottery, too, but you won't know unless you actually buy the ticket."

I was saved from having to one-up her analogy at the loud ringing of my door intercom. "Hang on, that's Nate with food," I said to Linn.

When I returned to my laptop after buzzing him up, Linn said perkily, "Let me talk to him."

"Not about..."

"No, don't be stupid," Linn scoffed. "Of course I'm not going to tell him we've been discussing him this whole time. I just like talking to him."

"Yeah, I know. I'm beginning to suspect you like him a lot more than you like me."

"Only beginning to?" she laughed.

"You suck. Oh, there he is," I said, when there was a smart rap at the door.

I ran over to open it, getting rewarded with a sweet kiss as Nate came in, bearing a large plastic bag of our evening sustenance.

We were likely visible in the webcam on my laptop, sat atop the kitchen's breakfast counter, but I didn't care this time. The nice thing about Linnea knowing about us, and thoroughly approving, was that I didn't feel like I had to keep anything under wraps and then throw myself into a massive swivet at the possibility of the wraps coming undone.

It was only in front of everybody else that I found great cause for divers alarums.

"Linn's on Skype," I said, relieving Nate of his burdens.

"Oh, great," he enthused, and commandeered the laptop over to the living room while I dealt with the cartons of Chinese in the kitchen.

Linnea was my one concession to Nate when it came to my battle of lassitude. She knew it, and he probably did too, which might partially explain why they had forged, within a single accidental Skype meeting weeks ago, a fast friendship almost as soon as introductions were over.

I usually tried not to listen in while they chatted unless I was invited to, but I suspected they were forming some kind of alliance against my stupidity. Occasionally I would hear one of them mention my name, followed by scattered laughter, which was proof enough.

It was a bit of a relief to find that Linn liked him so much, and vice versa, especially as she hadn't been Michelle's biggest fan by any stretch of the imagination, but it was something I was careful not to get used to. Linn liked him wholeheartedly and made a point of saying so often, but I couldn't count on her voice as the general consensus. For all I knew, she was the lone, crazy independent in a sea of single-party voters. True enough, her voice was loud, but she was only one.

"Emory," Nate called out. "Linn says bye."

"Bye," I shouted from the kitchen.

I grabbed plates and utensils, clattering them onto my small dining table, and Nate traipsed into the kitchen, pressing a quick kiss to my cheek as he passed by to wash his hands.

The familiarity with which he moved around me, in my home, was so unreservedly domestic that it caught me by surprise. It felt as though he had been here forever, and would always be somehow a part of this place and a part of my things.

It wasn't just that he knew his way around, not like a roommate or a frequent houseguest, it was that he moved like he belonged. And I wanted him to belong.

We sat down, picking our way through the contents of the cartons until our plates were filled and proportioned to our satisfaction.

"What do you and Linn even talk about?" I asked.

Nate grinned. "You."

"I knew it. About how unutterably awesome I am?" I said hopefully.

"Yeah, that's it," he said, chewing a dumpling thoughtfully. "Hit the nail right on the head there."

"And that is a bald-faced lie," I said.

He gave me an impish smile, which was corroboration enough. "She tells me incriminating things about you in case I need to use them against you later," he said, with no small amount of glee. "Needless to say, I quite love her."

"Well, this is alarming news. If you'll excuse me, I need to go and renounce our friendship now," I said, shifting in my seat as if to stand.

Laughing softly, Nate put a hand on my arm to keep me there. "She says you're pretty happy recently. With me," he said, a sudden touch of diffidence in his voice.

"Oh. Well, yeah. Did that not occur to you on your own?"

He shrugged, smiling. "It's nice to be told."

It struck me then, what Linn was doing. In all my dithering over how to articulate to other people what Nate meant to me, I had all but neglected to articulate it to him. Trust Linn to show my appreciation for him better than I could. She yells at me a lot, but she also looks out for me in ways I rarely even consider.

"Well," I said, "she's right."

"That usually seems to be the case."

We turned the conversation elsewhere for a while, talking about things that had happened at our respective workplaces, things we'd seen in the news, an Internet meme that had cracked Nate up for about five minutes straight.

Even as he tried to explain it to me, he had to keep stopping to laugh to himself and then apologize for laughing so much while I sat in amused bewilderment, the pieces of his anecdote missing all their connections. It was moments like this I lived for; reveling in the knowledge of the simple fact that I was able to share the minutiae of my life with someone who wanted to share his with me. We could be so interminably boring and so indescribably contented together.

Once dinner was finished and the dishes done and put away, we adjourned to the living room, as had become normal practice, to watch Season Two of *The Wire*, which Nate had been horrified to discover I had never seen.

His tastes ran along the same lines as mine did, so I turned out to like the show quite a bit, but at the moment I was having trouble concentrating on it, thinking of what Linnea had said to us both.

I *was* happy. Why couldn't I admit it to anyone else?

I looked over at Nate, the TV casting flickers and shadows over his profile, alternately sharpening the razor edges of his cheekbones and daubing away the nascent laugh lines at his eyes. *Mine*, I thought. It stirred something deeply sweet within me, and I couldn't believe I had never noticed how far gone I truly was.

Reaching over, I took Nate's hand, ran my fingertips over the crests of his knuckles, and pulled him slowly toward me. He came easily, compliant and curious, the look in his eyes softly expectant.

"I am really happy," I murmured against his lips, and I could feel a smile unfurling against mine. "With you."

I kissed him, and kissed him again, because I could, because I wanted to, because I was meant for nothing but this, even if nobody else knew it.

Chapter Ten

If anything could be described as a typical week, my week was it -- seeing clients, writing reports, spending time with Nate; nothing extraordinary, nothing to call attention to itself. In hindsight, this should have been sounding off all kinds of alarms in my head, because there is nothing the universe likes better than screwing with you five minutes after you've gotten your breath back from the last time it sauntered into town to make a mess of your life.

At least this time it had the decency to knock first.

I wended my way to the front door and peered through the peephole, at which point my stomach dropped several stories below, skittered out into traffic and got run over by a semi. My hand curled around the doorknob, but it took a few seconds before I managed to work up the fortitude to turn it.

"Michelle," I said, when I finally managed to pull the door open.

"Hi, Em," she said, her voice light and shuddery. She'd been crying, that much was obvious, her eyes red-rimmed and her nose bright enough to lead a reindeer brigade. There was a suitcase at her feet. "Can I come in?"

It would have been so utterly gratifying to simply slam the door in her face and walk away. Here was the scenario I'd imagined so many times in those early, angry days, nearly a year ago now, her standing before me, small and fragile, and I, the one left behind, with the power to break her with a single word.

I stepped out of the doorway, into the light of my apartment, and let her follow me in.

Michelle picked up her suitcase and slinked in, looking around the living room. "You redecorated."

"Yeah," I said tersely, unwilling to give up any further ground.

As noble as I felt for not giving in to the urge to turn her away, it quickly ebbed away in favor of irritation as she ran her fingers absently over pieces of my home that she used to know, that she used to be a part of. She always liked curling up in the blue armchair in the corner, used to disapprove of the habitually broken clock over my nonfunctional fireplace, loved watching the sunrise from the deck.

I knotted my arms over my chest, discarding the recollections. "Why are you here?"

She didn't appear to hear me, as she approached the armchair and picked up a pair of Nate's fingerless gloves, absent-mindedly left behind whenever he'd been here last. He was probably missing them; they matched his scarf. Michelle's face creased with bemusement.

"I thought you always hated these," she said with a small smile. "Every time you see someone wearing them you talk about how pointless they are."

It's true. I do think fingerless gloves are kind of pointless; when I said this to Nate he called me an old man and continued wearing them with impunity.

I looked away from the gloves and didn't say anything.

In my silence, comprehension dawned. "Ohh, these aren't yours. Are you-- Are you seeing someone?" she asked, her voice laced with equal parts accusation and amused disbelief.

"What? No. We're just friends," I said. Why was I lying? "Wait, why am I explaining myself to you? You *left*."

Michelle held her hands up in surrender. "I know, I know, I'm sorry. I didn't mean it to come out like that."

I sighed, rubbed a hand over my face. "What do you want?"

"Did you get my messages?"

"I deleted them," I said flatly.

"Oh. Okay." To my horror, her face suddenly crumpled and the tear tracks in her makeup deepened. "I'm so sorry, Em," she cried. "I was awful to you. What I did was inexcusable. You deserved so much better than that."

"Well, I won't argue with that," I said, and got a box of tissues for her, unsure whether I was obligated to provide any comfort beyond that, or whether I wanted to.

Despite my best efforts to systematically beat it into oblivion, a part of me still cared about her. She had inconvenienced me in a horrible way, and it would have been nice if she hadn't chosen our wedding day to do so, but see it from another side, from anyone else's eyes but mine, and here was a woman who'd had the courage to go after what made her happy. It was just that what made her happy didn't include me.

That same part of me wanted to put my arm around her, as I used to, and extinguish some of the hurt, even though I hurt too.

Michelle hiccupped, and dabbed delicately at her face with my proffered tissues. "I'm not asking you to forgive me; I know I don't deserve it," she said, once she'd gotten her breathing back under control.

I wasn't yet sure whether or not I agreed, so instead I sighed and said, "Let me get you some water."

Dutifully, I fetched a glass of water for her, and she took it with gratitude radiating from every pore.

"You've always been good to me, Em," she said, a crack in her voice threatening to break the dam again. She took a deep breath. "That's why I broke up with Will."

"Oh, Christ," I said, taking several agitated steps away, my living room suddenly way too small to contain all this.

Well, hell. If Plucky Heroine and Good-Looking Bastard can't make it, what chance do the rest of us second bananas have?

"I broke up with Will because I realized I was still in love with you," she said in a small voice.

"Michelle," I said sharply from the other end of the room. "On our wedding day, you left me at the altar because you realized you were still in love with *him*." If there was a way to punctuate every single letter of every single word I would have.

She took an urgent step forward to disabuse me of my apparent misapprehensions but stopped when I threw a forbidding hand up. The room was already feeling close enough.

"I was in love with the idea of him," she said. "I mean, he could sweep me off my feet like nobody's business, but... Em, you were the one who was always there for me, and I didn't know-- I didn't realize how important that was until afterward."

I shook my head. "So, what? You're here to win me back? You think you can just waltz in here and cry all over me and then everything will magically be fine?"

"No," she said quietly. "I know I hurt you really badly, and believe me, I'll regret that for the rest of my life. I'd do anything to make it up to you."

"Well, you're just going to have to discover time travel, then. Good luck with that," I said curtly, and stalked to the front door, intent on showing her the way out.

"Em. Please," she said, her voice breaking, which then broke something in me.

It's not fair that people can do this to other people, a crack in her voice and I was in shards again. Having feelings is exhausting. I wouldn't recommend having them, it you can avoid it.

"What do you want from me?" I asked, my hand slipping from the doorknob.

"A chance. To fix everything I broke, to start over."

I shook my head, uncomprehending. "Start over?"

"Just let me be in your life again," she amended. "I miss you, Em."

Michelle took a tentative step forward, and when I didn't make her stop this time, tried another, inching toward me carefully as if I was strapped with explosives liable to go off any second. It was a fair assessment, in a way.

"We were good together, once," she said softly. "We could be again."

Could we? Did I owe it to myself to try? I had almost married her once, been prepared to pledge the rest of my life to her. How much did that count for now?

"I can't do this right now," I said. It was too much all at once; my head was a churning mess of too many questions that I had no answers for, and my heart felt even worse.

"Okay," Michelle said. "Okay, that's fine. You need time, that's fine."

"Yeah," I said. "You should probably go."

She bit her lip. "Actually, um, I was wondering if I could stay here for a little while?" she said, squeezing her fingers, a nervous tic I recognized from long ago. "I mean, not forever, obviously. I'm going to start looking for apartments tomorrow. I-- I don't have anywhere else to go right now."

My head fell back, and I silently pleaded with the ceiling for help. "You're really asking a hell of a lot of me right now, Michelle," I said finally, when the cavalry failed to arrive.

"I know, I'm sorry," she said for the millionth time. "I literally bought the first plane ticket here that I could get; there's practically nothing in my suitcase. The moment I realized what an idiot I was I just wanted to come to you, and... say everything I said."

"There's this thing called the telephone. All the kids are using it."

"You won't answer my calls."

As far as grand gestures went, this one was up there, an old standby, flying across the country on an impulse because your heart is too full to hold your feelings in any longer. In the movie of my life, this scene would probably be a lot more romantic, or a lot more tempestuous, depending on where the director wanted to go with this couple, because the screenwriter obviously had no idea what he was doing, nothing but blank pages from this point forward.

In the reality of my life, this scene was just quietly, back-breakingly exhausting.

"Did you envision this going differently?" I asked.

Her lips lifted into a mirthless smile. "I hoped it would. I'd hoped -- foolishly, I know -- that even after what I'd done, you would still love me." She searched my face, and something in it persuaded her to push her luck. "Do you?"

I shoved away from the door, turning away from her. "You can take the couch. You know where the linen closet is; there are extra blankets in there," I said brusquely, striding to my bedroom and closing the door tight behind me.

All this time I had been so focused on the possibility of creating something new with Nate, it hadn't even occurred to me that there might still be something lingering to recreate with Michelle.

I thought I had shed all the memories, all the joys and pains associated with her, but it turned out I had only crammed them into the deepest, darkest recesses of my mind, where they had just been waiting all along for a moment like this.

Everything I thought I had gotten over was suddenly flooding back, and the force of it was staggering.

***

Like the mature, responsible adult that I was, I started avoiding Michelle at home by claiming an unusually heavy caseload at the clinic, and avoiding Nate everywhere else by inventing an illness. I wasn't proud of it, but there seemed very few alternatives available, other than giving in to the welling panic that I barely had a lid on, and I soldiered through the next couple of days with my head firmly stuck in the sand.

To make at least some part of the lie a little less of a lie, I took to pottering around the clinic after hours, going through all my reports with a fine-toothed comb, paging through some of the old textbooks stashed around my office, reading newly published journal articles. By the time I left, I was incredibly well informed, but that did little to assuage the sick churning in my stomach, knowing I would be opening my apartment door to the sight of Michelle in it.

She had been there for a few days now, tiptoeing around me at first, unsure of where her place was, but after a little while, realizing I wasn't on the verge of throwing her out, she seemed to settle in a little bit.

It was bad enough that she had turned up at all, worse still that I somehow found it within me to let her stay. But worst of all was that she settled in in the way she used to, her familiarity draped all over the apartment, old habits come back in full force -- the way she'd plump up a couch cushion after sitting for a while, the spiral of hair that would wind around her finger when she was engrossed in a television program, how she liked to tuck her feet under when reading a book.

If it hadn't been for Nate's imprints all over the place, his distinct belonging, it would have almost been like she had never left at all. Maybe that was her whole plan, to simply impress her presence back into my life until I forgot the difference.

I couldn't bring myself to shut her out completely, but neither did I want to let her back into my life again, at least not without some kind of cathartic mock trial in which I'd play both charismatic prosecutor and cranky judge, as well as all twelve of the jury. I didn't have the nerve to simply sit down and talk it out with her, and I definitely harbored no designs on bringing Nate into it.

It wasn't that I didn't expect it all to catch up to me, but I had been hoping, futilely as it turned out, that it wouldn't be quite so soon. Or quite so horribly.

"Hey, Em," Michelle said, when I lumbered in late in the evening, having eaten a vending machine dinner at the clinic to get out of the possibility of having to dine with her.

"Hi," I said shortly.

"A friend of yours stopped by earlier. Um, Nate, I think?" she said, looking up at me from the couch, her makeshift bed still.

If I had been carrying anything at that point, I would have dropped it. "What?" I rasped.

"Oh," she said, looking off to the left in consultation with her memory. "I think that's what he said his name was. Dark hair, brown eyes?"

"Yeah, that's--" I said with some difficulty, finding it extremely hard to breathe all of a sudden. "I know who he is. Did he-- What did he say?"

"Nothing really," Michelle reported. "I guess he just came by to see if you were home. He kind of left in a hurry, though. I don't know him from before; is he someone from work or something?"

I stared at her, incapable of forming a coherent reply. Giving up, I said nothing at all, and instead turned away and locked myself in my bedroom.

Oh god.

Oh fuck.

I tugged my cell phone from my pocket and speed-dialed Nate, swearing up an electric blue storm of curses in my head, most of them directed at my stupid, unbelievably stupid self. The phone rang and rang, connecting at last to Nate's voicemail. I hung up without leaving a message and cursed myself again.

I tried a few more times throughout the rest of the night, but the speed with which I kept getting sent to voicemail made it all too clear that Nate was deliberately ignoring my calls.

It was pointless leaving a message; what could I say? How could I even begin to explain myself within the allotted three minutes of voicemail?

Fuck.

And furthermore, *fuck*.

I kept my phone close as I climbed into bed, heartsick, willing it to ring, willing Nate's picture to turn up on my display. It didn't work, and I fell into a fitful sleep, waking what seemed like every thirty seconds to check if I had accidentally missed a phone call, but each frantic inspection met with disappointment.

Morning rolled around, shining bright through my windows with callous abandon. It was to be an unseasonably warm weekend; there would doubtless be plenty of people out enjoying it while I remained steadfastly rooted to my mattress, holding my phone and wishing to any deity willing to listen that I get a chance to fix this.

My phone rang. Startled, I nearly hurled it across the room but managed to get myself under control and pick up the call instead.

"Nate," I said, clutching the phone close to my ear.

Dispensing with ceremony and any attempts at sounding any less pissed off than he was, Nate asked a curt, "Are you home?"

"Yeah."

"Is she there?"

"No," I said, remembering having heard the telltale sounds of her getting up, having a quick breakfast and slipping out the door. "Um, she's out all day apartment hunting, I think."

"Fine. I'm coming over," he said, and hung up.

Tossing my phone on the bed, where it skipped toward a pillow now that it could finally get some rest after I'd been working it all night, I leapt out and ransacked my closet. I wanted to look presentable, at least, while I pleaded my case, in something a little more acceptable than boxers and a T-shirt with a hole in the armpit. What kind of thing do you wear to plead your case in? A suit?

Fuck.

I scrubbed my face with a hasty palm and took a long, calming breath, letting my anxieties leach out of me as I let the air out through my nose. I threw on a normal set of clothes and went out to the living room to wait.

As I had suspected, Michelle was out, though the visible detritus of her presence throughout the room -- suitcase, blankets, a pair of heels -- made it impossible to pretend that she hadn't been here. In my fluster, I had made drastic plans to try to convince Nate he had simply imagined the whole encounter, but it was just as well that I didn't dig my grave even deeper by feeding him yet another lie.

It occurred to me then that I was a fucking terrible person, and Nate's sharp knock on the door only drove the point home.

I opened it, and he stalked in, his face cold and impassive.

"This isn't what you think," was my choice of an opening gambit, which only added to my collection in a long string of poor decisions.

Nate ground his teeth. "She's been here for *days*, and you've been canceling all your plans with me, pretending to be sick the whole time. What the hell am I supposed to think?"

"That I can't, in good conscience, throw somebody out into the street?" I proposed. "Look, she just turned up, completely unexpectedly, the other day, with no place to stay, and there was all this crying, okay? And I can't-- And then she said she wanted to work things out, and I couldn't--"

He held up a hand to stop my drivel. "She wants to work things out?" he said, blinking at me in disbelief.

I got the feeling that that was going to be a sticking point. "I mean, I-- That's-- Yeah, she said that, yes."

His arms folded over his chest tightly, as though that was the only thing keeping him together, and he started pacing. "And what did you say?"

"I don't-- I didn't say anything."

It was entirely possible that I might have said something, maybe even something profound, but whatever it was had clearly decided not to hang around in my memory banks. Things were already bizarre enough; trying to wrap my mind around them was impossible, to say nothing of being able to remember anything I'd uttered in the moment when Michelle had turned up at my doorstep and turned my head inside out.

"You didn't say anything," Nate echoed, and if I was supposed to understand the meaning behind the reiteration, then I was failing very badly.

"What do you want me to say?"

"I want you to tell me the fucking truth, Emory."

"I am," I insisted.

Nate stopped pacing, shot me a sharp glance; something steely glinted in his eye. He drew himself up, almost imperceptibly. "Fine then, I want you to tell *her* the fucking truth," he said.

"What?"

"You haven't, have you?" he said, not so much a question as a dare.

I turned from the heat of his glare, and I didn't say anything. There was a good chance I would remember my silence this time around, the pinpoint moment a crack appeared in his heart, the moment I put it there.

"Christ," Nate muttered to himself, rubbing a hand over his face. When his hand fell back to his side, his mouth twisted with scorn. "Let me see if I have this straight. Michelle shows up, you take her in. She wants you back, and you conveniently neglect to tell her you're already in a relationship. Is that right? Is that what's happening?"

"What-- *No*," I said. "It's not like that. It's not that simple."

"Then explain it to me," he gritted. "Explain to me why it's so hard for you to tell your ex to find a goddamn hotel. And why it's so hard for you to admit that you even like me. Or, hell, you don't even have to admit that you like me, just that you occasionally enjoy fucking me."

"That's not fair," I protested. "That is not fair. Nate, I am not like you."

A sullen laugh tumbled past his lips. "What, gay?"

I had intended to say something along the lines of not having the same kind of courage he obviously possessed, even long ago when he'd been half my age now, but what came out instead was, "You're not even allowed to go home for the holidays."

He turned sharply to me. "No, I'm not. But that's their choice," he said firmly. "And I made the choice to be true to who I am. I'm not going to try to change that just because it's inconvenient for somebody else."

"You think that's what this is?"

"Isn't it?" His jaw shifted tensely. "You only seem happy to be with me when no one else is around."

"That's not true."

"Then why haven't you told Michelle?" When I had no answer for that, Nate nodded bitterly and went on, "Let me take a stab at it, then. She's safe for you, she's familiar and, more importantly, acceptable. And when this invariably becomes too much for you, and you decide to cut and run, you're going to run straight to her. She's your back-up plan."

Angry indignation flared in my chest suddenly. "Don't," I said, raising a warning finger. "Don't pretend like you even know anything about me and Michelle."

Despite my tone, his face softened a fraction. "I know she left you at the altar to run off with someone else. Isn't that enough?"

"It's not that simple," I said again, wracking my mind to find a way to make him understand.

We had a history, Michelle and I. We'd had a life together, we were going to spend the rest of it together. And despite what I had said, Nate had hit at least somewhere in the near vicinity of the truth -- that Michelle was what my life was supposed to have been. It would've been a nice life; it still could be.

With Nate, I had no idea. I couldn't imagine what sixty years down the road would look like for us, but neither could I imagine the next sixty years without him.

"Yes, it is," Nate insisted. He carded his fingers through his hair, frustrated, adamant in his rectitude. "God, you know what? This isn't even about me or Michelle. It's about you being too scared to see the truth, and too scared to ask everyone around you to see it too."

I shook my head, tired of him acting as if he knew me better than I did, tired of this fight. I didn't want to see where it would go. "That's not even-- Christ, Nate, what are you even talking about?"

A fist still in his hair, Nate's knuckles whitened, what was left of his patience in shreds. "You're *gay*, Emory!" he shouted. "Or-- Or bi. Or, fuck, whatever you want to call it that isn't straight. I know you desperately wish you could be, but when you have sex with a man and you like it, that should give you a pretty good fucking clue!"

His chest rose and fell with the exertion of the outburst, and I could only stare at him, cold and furious.

"Stop," he said, when calm returned to him. "Please-- Stop pretending to be something you're not."

For some reason his softened tone infuriated me more than any of his shouting had. "Don't come in here," I ground out, "and preach all this self-actualization bullshit at me, all right? You don't know what the fuck you're talking about."

"*I* don't--" Nate threw up his hands. "Fine. Fine. Call me when you get your head out of your ass," he snapped, stalking toward the door.

When he got there, he stopped suddenly, struck by a new thought. With his hand on the doorknob, he tilted his head back, blinking rapidly. He sucked in a shaky breath. When he spoke again, he barely looked in my direction, but underneath the glow of the light in the hall, I could see that his lashes were wet.

"No," he said softly. "You know what? Don't call. I can't keep doing this with you and waiting for you to make up your mind."

"Nate," I said, with the kind of cautious voice you'd use when somebody is teetering on the ledge of a tall building; he was going jump, and he was going to do it without me.

He looked at me then, his face stricken, and it sent a stab of agony through my heart. I had made him hurt that way and I hated myself for it, even as I hated him for putting me through the same.

"Since this is so hard for you, let me make it easier. You want to be with Michelle? Go ahead. Do whatever the hell you want; you have my blessing," he said with a resentful smile. A tear sleeted down his cheek and he didn't bother wiping it away. "You don't have to keep this dirty little secret anymore. Consider me permanently out of the picture."

Ten minutes after he slammed the door behind him, I was still standing in the same spot, staring at my unmoving front door, willing him to come back.

Chapter Eleven

Nate didn't come back that day, nor the next. And by the end of the week it was starting to look like he wasn't planning on coming back ever.

They say absence makes the heart grow fonder, which is all well and good, but nobody ever mentions the part about absence making the heart splinter into a million little fragments so absolutely that all you're left with is dust in its place.

That was where I was now, a week without Nate, a week knowing that in my passive-aggressive pursuit for self-preservation I had destroyed our relationship, a week of nothing-dust where my heart should be. Missing it didn't help it hurt any less; it burned like an abscess burned, the larger the void, the more it hurt.

I holed up in my room whenever possible, still taking pains to avoid Michelle. If she suspected anything of my self-imprisonment, she probably attributed it to me still trying to wrap my head around her return, which was at least half true. The other half was that I resented her return, resented her for leaving in the first place and for setting everything in motion to the bookends of my heartbreak.

And still, knowing she was just on the other side of the door made some sad, nostalgic part of me want to seek her out like I used to, to listen to her soothe me with tired comforts of everything turning out okay in the end. I knew it was a bad idea, so I didn't, but the notion was there all the same.

I couldn't fathom making things go back to the way they were with her; there were too many broken pieces to find and too much to bury, but that didn't stop me from wondering anyway. We had been happy before, hadn't we?

But Nate and I had been happy too.

"At least he didn't say 'it's not you, it's me'," I mumbled to Linn when I caught her on Skype on the sixth Nate-less day, pulling the cuffs of my sweatshirt over my hands and rubbing my eyes, making the dark circles even darker. I probably looked deranged.

"Yeah," Linn said kindly. "Because it's definitely you."

I removed my hands temporarily to glare at the screen. "Hey, you're supposed to be on my side."

"I am, dude," Linn said. "You know I love you more than my own brother. Which is kind of why I'm obligated to tell you that you fucked up."

I let out the long groan of a dying beast. "I know. I know I did." I looked up at the screen, where Linnea was gently dandling her baby in her arms, and added, "Hey, shouldn't you cover her ears if you're going to swear at me?"

Linn gave me a flat look. "We live in Scotland. Chances are, she's going to have twice my repertoire of curse words before she's six. Tristan said 'shit' to me the other day; he's not even two."

"Oh, well, you might as well give her a head start, then," I said.

"Yeah, I mean, she's going to want to keep up with her big brother, right?" She turned to her precious little girl, touching their noses together, and cooed, "Your idiot Uncle Emory fucked up with Uncle Nate. Yes, he did. Yes, he did."

The baby laughed, the heartless little thing.

The corners of my mouth pulled downward. "Hey, you barely even know each other. How come he gets to be an uncle too?"

"Because I like him. And because you want him to be," she said simply.

I frowned into the webcam, disconcerted.

"Why? Why are you making this face at me? This isn't breaking news, Em," she said. "You've been in love with him practically since you met."

"I don't-- I don't believe in love at first sight," I said churlishly.

"I'm not talking about love at first sight; I'm talking about you being happier in however many months you've known him than... god, since I've known *you*."

"What?"

Linn rolled her eyes dramatically; any further and she'd snap a tendon. "You were *happy*. Like Christmas morning happy. Like..."

I cocked my head, waiting for her to go on.

She made a wild gesture, agitatedly searching for the right analogy that would penetrate my feeble mind. "Like manifesting a dream you've had your whole life happy. Like thank god I can stop searching because I found him happy. Like I never knew I was missing a part of myself until now happy."

"Oh," I said. So that's what that was.

"Y'know, before you screwed it all up."

"And I thank you for that reminder."

"I was already planning your big gay wedding, you know," she said, somewhat accusatorily. "It would've been amazing."

As she delineated her amazing plans, describing things in Tuscan red and champagne, the fog of doubt and irresolution in my mind cleared for a blissful second. It wasn't an image of anything Linnea was saying, because hell if I knew what a pomander was, but one of me and Nate, dapper and nervous in tuxes and in front of an officiant.

The picture came so naturally to me I could have cried.

At the moment I couldn't even remember what color a vest I had been wearing on my real wedding day, but this I could see, down to the stitches on Nate's lapels, and the light of his smile. God, I ached for that smile.

"Please let me plan this wedding for you," Linn said. "Go and grovel, and be happy."

And yet. "What about Michelle?"

Linn groaned a gigantic groan of frustration, which thoroughly bewildered the baby. "Emory Archibald James," she said, channeling all exasperated mothers the world over, pointing a stern finger at me.

I squinted into the webcam. "That's not even my name."

That took the wind out of her sails. She looked at the screen, perplexed. "What? Really? That's what I always say when I imagine myself yelling at you. That's not your middle name? Are you sure?"

I gave her a look that I hoped would appropriately convey how insane I thought she was, which was extremely. "It's Anthony."

She let this information digest for a moment, mouthing both versions of my name to herself, and shook her head. "No," she decided. "Archibald has a nicer ring to it."

"There are many things wrong with you, including the fact that you think Archibald is in some way an acceptable name for a living person," I said, though I gestured for her to carry on.

"Emory Archibald James," she said evenly, "you don't owe her anything. And you don't owe the old you anything either. What you owe yourself, Emory James, in this moment, is to go after what makes you happy. And I think you know exactly what that is."

I did, and it was terrifying in its sudden clarity.

Funny little things, epiphanies. Sometimes they ambush you from the shadows, sometimes they just trail alongside quietly until you realize one day they've been there the whole time, simply waiting for you to turn and notice.

I definitely noticed now, though it would have been helpful if it had at least tapped me on the shoulder before I had completely ruined things with Nate.

"Your kids are lucky to have a mom like you," I said after a while.

Linn smiled. "Yeah, I know, I'm totally kick-ass, right?" she said, and laughed the mock arrogance away. "Can I record you saying that? Then I'll have proof to show them that at least one person said it when they turn teenagers and hate me for the next ten years."

"I'll put in a good word," I said. "And they will believe me because as someone who is not their parent, they'll never stop thinking I'm cool."

"Yeah... *cool*," she said skeptically. "Let's go with that."

***

"Oh my god, Em," was the first thing out of Michelle's mouth when I admitted to her that I had been seeing Nate, owner of the mysterious, pointless, fingerless gloves and a sizable chunk of my heart.

"Did I-- Did I turn you gay?" was, regrettably, the second thing.

I looked at her askance. "Okay, say that again, just in your head this time, and then tell me whether you really want me to answer that."

Michelle stared for a moment, and then shook her head at herself. "Sorry, sorry. I'm... surprised, I guess. I kind of thought-- I thought we had a shot," she said, directing a rueful glance at the floor.

"Once," I said. It wasn't meant to be unkind, just true.

We would've had a nice life, me and Michelle. Maybe a house with a fenced yard in the suburbs, a dog to ruin that yard, some impossible fraction of children; it would've been pleasant. And that's all it would have been at its best, if that best was something we could even hope to achieve. I couldn't trust her unreservedly with my heart anymore as I once had. A shred of doubt would always hang between us, because although forgiveness comes with time, forgetting doesn't. Besides, I couldn't entrust my heart to her because it was already in someone else's keeping.

I was giving up a nice life for the possibility of a great one, damn the consequences. Me and Nate -- I had the feeling that we had a chance to be truly happy. And he already came with a dog.

Michelle shifted her feet awkwardly. "So... I guess I should probably get out of your hair, huh?" she said, and started to gather some of her things that had gotten strewn around the living room.

"Hey," I said, "if you need to crash here a little longer..."

"No, this was a mistake," Michelle muttered. She lifted her head, a book clutched in one hand, her eyes closed as she attempted to compose herself. She smiled at me when she opened them. "No, it wasn't a mistake. You were worth the try."

"Uh. Thank you," I said, taking full possession of the awkwardness in the room now. It fit me like a glove, a proper one.

"Em," she said, squeezing my hand, "everyone should be so lucky as to have you in their lives. I just realized it too late. You deserve someone who knew that from the first minute he saw you. He did, right? This Nate of yours?"

This Nate of mine. My mind reeled in a litany of memories of all that Nate had said and done when we had been in Thailand, when we had returned to our real worlds; maybe it would have been clear then, too, to someone a little more observant than I was. He had been trying to tell me all along.

"Yeah, I think so," I said.

"Good," Michelle said. "That's really good, Em."

We got her packed and put in a cab, and though I offered once more to let her stay until her new lease started, she had none of it, opting for a hotel instead. We hugged goodbye, and I stood on the empty sidewalk, watching the cab take her away to wherever in her life she was going, swallowed into the stream of city traffic.

***

It occurred to me one morning that any day now I would be required to forswear any old allegiances to the The Other Guy Club and turn in my membership card.

My life had somehow veered into Good-Looking Bastard territory, all chaos and meaningless chatter up till the point when realization had come upon me like a sack of bricks -- otherwise known as that one time Linnea shouted at me.

(Not to be confused with that one other time Linnea yelled at me. Be on the receiving end of her pointy finger enough times and you learn to distinguish the finer subtleties.)

It was Nate who made me happy, and I'd been stupid enough to not notice. Never mind the Good-Looking; I was just, plainly and simply, Bastard, and I needed to get it together, needed to get him back.

I didn't have a grand plan to win him back.

Tradition dictated that I should do it in a hugely public way, preferably with a microphone and backup band involved, so that there would be enough witnesses for him to feel really awkward about saying no.

But chances were I'd get more embarrassed about the whole thing much, much earlier than he would. Plus, I'd always considered such public displays a cheap substitute anyway, showy but essentially lacking in substance. They are the fingerless gloves of relationships.

Instead, I invited Hal over to play video games with me.

It was after I underwent two solid trouncings at kart racing that I finally brought Nate up. That way, if Hal happened to storm out with the intention of never speaking to me again, he could at least leave our very last gaming session together on an otherwise high note. It's the little things.

"So, uh, do you remember Nate? From the Super Bowl party?" I asked, in what I hoped sounded like a casual tone of voice.

"Super Bowl party. Tall, thin?" Hal said. Something clicked into place inside his head, and he added, pleased with himself for remembering, "Not from the speech clinic."

"Yeah, that's the one. He wasn't from the speech clinic," I said. I let my guy careen right off the racetrack to certain doom, and put the controller down so I could rub nervous palms on my jeans. "Um. We, uh... We were sort of-- We were seeing each other for a while. Like, dating."

"Like?" Hal said.

"Dating," I clarified at last, decisively, and braced myself for whatever blow was headed my way.

Hal flipped his controller onto the couch and stretched. "Yeah, I kind of already knew," he said through a yawn.

My stomach unclenched, and I blinked at him. "What?"

"Super Bowl party," he explained, setting the scene. "You cut yourself and I went to your bathroom for bandages. There were two toothbrushes in there.

Plus, there was this whole weird vibe between the two of you the entire time."

"Seriously?" I wheezed. "Are you actually serious?"

He'd known all this time. After all that anxiety, all the sleepless nights I'd gone through over telling him, this was how he repaid me? I could have punched him in the face.

"Why didn't you say anything?" I demanded.

He shrugged. "You didn't."

"Okay, that is a fair point. I will give you that," I conceded. "And... you don't care?"

"Nah, he seems cool. I mean, you like him, right?"

"Yes," I said, carefully watching his expression.

Hal shrugged again, his face changing not an iota. "Then okay."

I grinned, infinitely grateful for his easy understanding. "Hal," I said, overflowing with goodwill as I clapped him on the shoulder, "I am glad we are friends."

He eyed me suspiciously. "You're not going to make us hug or anything, are you?"

"Good lord, no," I said. "To show my appreciation, I will let you win this next round."

"Yeah," Hal laughed, picking up his controller again and selecting our next challenge. "You keep telling yourself that, buddy."

Chapter Twelve

With the first phase of what I realized had become my grand plan successfully conquered, I set my sights higher for the next round.

Until I got through this I had no business trying to get Nate back. My fears, my apprehensiveness had been the driving factors in making Nate go away in the end, and unless I wanted that hanging over my head forever, I had to find out, one way or another, what telling the truth would bring.

It wasn't for Nate, at least not exclusively for Nate. Regardless of whether or not he was in my life, it was still something I had to face for myself and with as much honesty as I could muster. Nate was only the catalyst in all this; I had to be the one to pull the trigger.

When my lunch break came around, I reached for the phone to call my parents.

The phone rang as soon as I touched the receiver, startling me into rolling a few inches away in my desk chair. Clipping my hands to the edge of the desk, I dragged myself back and picked up the call, rattling off the standard office welcome.

"Petersen Speech Clinic, Emory James speaking."

"Hi, Emory," said a voice I couldn't quite place. "It's, um, Julie, Abby Montgomery's mom? She used to come to you for her esses?"

"Of course. Hi," I said, slightly disconcerted that Nate's sister of all people would be calling at this precise moment.

I suppose that for the sake of true serendipity, I would've preferred that it be Nate himself on the other end, but you take what you can get when the universe decides to move in mysterious ways.

"What can I do for you, Julie?"

"Um," she said, and I heard the intake of a shaky breath. "It's our father-- Um, Nate's and my father? He had a heart attack and passed away early yesterday."

"Oh my god," I said, stunned. "I'm so sorry."

"The memorial service is tomorrow," she continued, her voice steadier now. "I think it would mean a lot to Nate if you were able to come."

"I-- I would love to-- I mean," I amended, mentally slapping myself. "I mean, I really appreciate the opportunity to pay my respects to your father, but you know that Nate and I aren't... We're not, um... We haven't spoken in a while."

"I know," said Julie. "And I know it's short notice; it's out of state and you'd have to fly out, and... It's just that I think he could really use a friendly face."

It hit me then, what she really meant. After nearly fifteen years of staying as far away as he could, Nate was finally going back home, going home to carry a casket.

"I'll be there," I said.

After writing down the details, I got online to book an air ticket and a hotel room, and went out to the front desk to inform Marybeth of my impending departure.

"Marybeth, hi," I said, barely waiting for her to acknowledge me. "I have to cancel all my Friday appointments. Tomorrow's appointments. Um, emergency."

She gave me a look of deep concern. "Oh no, is everything okay?"

"Yeah, yeah, fine," I said, trying to keep my tone light. "I have to fly out to a memorial service tomorrow, and then I guess the burial is on Sunday."

"Oh, I'm so sorry. Who passed?"

I had been hoping she wouldn't ask, but of course she would ask. She was a kind and caring person with a vested interest in all of our well-beings, and at the moment I very much wished she would stop.

"It's..." I said, and decided that if it had to come out sometime, it might as well be now. "My boyfriend's father."

Technically, not true, but saying ex-boyfriend would have made it sound even less like a real reason, and I was already having enough trouble with this conversation as it was.

Even without the inclusion of the prefixal distinction, the look she directed at me this time was one of deep suspicion. "What? Honey," she said, raising a disapproving eyebrow. "Usually when people want to take a long weekend, they go with a grandmother's funeral. Are you sure you've thought this through?"

I sighed. "Look, it's a long story. You remember my articulation case from a few months ago, Abby Montgomery? About yea high?"

Marybeth nodded, her eyes still narrowed as she acknowledged my hand gesture.

"Okay," I said, buoyed. "You remember she used to sometimes come in with her uncle? Tall, super handsome?"

"Yes. The girls and I always loved Monday and Thursday afternoons for that," Marybeth said, and her expression gradually changed to one of surprise as it all sank in. "Are you telling me that you and him...?"

"Yeah, me and him. We-- Yes. And only well after I discharged Abby," I hastily clarified, preempting any further eyebrow action. "Look, you can call Abby's mom if you want; we still have all their contact information on file. Besides, it was Julie who called me not ten minutes ago to tell me about the funeral."

She leaned forward, gazing at me curiously, almost proud. "No, no, I believe you. It would be such a stupid story to make up otherwise, but it's you."

"Uh, thank you?" I said, not at all sure what she meant.

"Good for you, hon," she said, outright grinning now. "No wonder you were smiling like such an idiot all the time. And now that I think about it, the two of you? I bet you look nice together."

"Okay..." I said, feeling more awkward than ever. "Um, please help me cancel my appointments for tomorrow?"

Marybeth nodded. "Done."

"Thank you," I said. I turned on my heel to return to my office, but then ended up making a full swivel to face her again. "And please don't tell anybody."

"Okay."

"No, actually," I said, giving up the ghost of a past me, "tell anybody you want. I mean, if people are going to talk about me, I might as well do them the courtesy of being away while they do it, right?"

"I think that's wise," Marybeth said, pointing a pen at me. "Snag yourself a guy like that, you definitely shouldn't be keeping it to yourself."

It was enough to make me laugh. "Thanks, Marybeth," I said.

I turned again, making it all the way back to my office this time to finish up the rest of my reports with an occasionally wandering mind.

I hoped Julie had made the right call by getting in touch with me and inviting me to the memorial service. With Nate doubtless in an already brittle emotional place, I wasn't sure if seeing me would make it any easier on him.

After all, as he had so succinctly predicted, I had turned out to be the heartbreaker in our equation; I hadn't believed him then -- I mean, look at me. A single yellow school pencil is already difficult enough for me to snap in two, let alone break someone as resilient as Nate. And yet I had managed to do it anyway.

Go me.

Still, I had to go to the service. I wanted to be there in whatever capacity he needed me, even if it was to have somebody to yell at. And if he didn't want me there, then that was fine; I was prepared for that possibility too.

It was a long night, tosses and turns come to disturb me for hours on end as I lay in bed, wondering what Nate was feeling, what he was doing. Getting more sleep than I was, with any luck.

From what Julie had intimated, Nate would already have arrived in his North Carolinian hometown by now. Would he have gone to see his mom right away? Would it just be a reprise of the rift they had created years ago?

As ineffectual as it was, I closed my eyes and concentrated on the image of him, sad and alone out there, sending him what little strength I could through the ether.

With that, he could at least break an extra pencil if he wanted. Every little bit counts, right?

By the time I fell asleep, it was time to get up.

The bulk of my flight, thankfully a relatively short jaunt, was spent in a state of nervous agitation, and making sure I could see a corner of the airsickness bag in the seat pocket in front, in case of emergency hyperventilation or worse.

Even though my intentions were to head out to the service for Nate and not for me, there was no stopping the way my stomach kept twisting in anticipation of seeing him again.

If Julie was right and he was happy to see me, then maybe we would still have a chance at something after all. But if she wasn't, then it would simply be the end. That wasn't a thought I particularly relished entertaining, but it was one I needed to brace myself for.

Not having Nate around for the past couple of weeks had been hellish in its utter emptiness. Work provided a sufficient distraction during daylight hours, but it was in the quiet, in the dark, when there was nothing to keep me company except the thoughts I lashed at myself, that it was nearly unbearable.

Up until now I at least had the treacherous hope that there was still a chance of things working out, that maybe he might knock on my door one day and say that all was forgiven. I still had that hope for at least a few more hours, and I cradled it close, for all the good it would do.

The plane landed without incident, and I got my rental car and headed to the hotel, changing quickly into a black suit.

I inspected myself in the bathroom mirror; I looked exactly like what a caricaturist might draw of someone who'd recently suffered the twin misfortunes of heartache and insomnia. If this was what I had looked like in Thailand as well, Nate seriously needed to make an appointment with his optometrist as soon as possible, because there was nothing remotely resembling cute in this face.

Splashing a handful of cold water over it in the hopes of looking at least slightly less like a dues-paying member of the local undead chapter, I steeled myself for whatever may come, and headed for the funeral home and, ultimately, my reckoning.

Once I reached the funeral home and parked my car, I stayed seated in it for a while, watching an erratic stream of visitors trickle in solemn-faced, wanting the safety net of being lost in the crowd if I ended up needing it. I didn't see Nate or Julie; they had probably been inside for a while.

Finally, with two minutes left, according to the digital display in the car, to the start of the service, I let myself out.

Inside, most of the guests were already seated. I took a program but avoided the guestbook. The picture of Nate's father on the program had obviously been taken in his later years, but immediately I could see the traits Nate had taken from him -- the lean build, the dark, deep-set eyes, the line of his jaw. Nate's heart, however, was all his own.

Hovering in the far back of the room, I spied Nate in the front row with Julie, Abby and an older, gray-haired woman I assumed was his mother. They said all of nothing to one another, but I hoped at least that his being seated with his family was a good sign.

Everybody went through the appropriate motions -- music, speeches, readings of Bible passages to ease the hearts of those left behind. I learned more about Nate's dad from the variety of remembrance speeches presented over the course of an hour than I had ever heard from Nate in months, but nobody in the room learned about Mr. Harris from Nate's eyes.

But I guess a memorial service isn't really the best time to talk about a father who didn't love his son enough.

Once the closing prayer was finished, the guests began getting up and adjourning to a nearby room for the reception, a few of them making quiet remarks to the family on their way past. I remained in my spot in the last row, waiting and watching, until almost no one was left.

Julie spotted me as she passed toward the reception. She gave me a nod and a small smile, which I returned, and indicated with a tilt of her head that it was probably okay for me to unglue myself from the back row.

She quietly took Abby in one hand, and her mother on the other arm, out of the room, and then there was just me left, and Nate in the front, his hunched back to me, elbows heavy on his knees as he stared up at the wreathed photo of his father behind the podium.

I took a deep breath, swallowed the anxiety that had knotted in my throat, and walked toward the front of the room, sitting a couple of seats away from him.

"You look a lot like him," I said, as gently as I could.

Nate's head snapped up at the sound of my voice, his face a shambles of too many emotions to name. "What are you doing here?"

"Julie called me yesterday," I said.

Something fiery crossed his face, though I couldn't tell whether he was grateful that I had come, or if he was pissed at Julie for interfering in his life. It didn't help that he chose not to say anything in response, only went back to leaning on his knees, the fire petered out as quickly as it had flared up.

"For what it's worth," I tried again, "I'm really sorry about your dad."

He acknowledged the sentiment with a short nod. His fingers were twined, turning white in places where he was gripping too hard.

"She won't talk to me," he said to the floral carpet.

I didn't have to ask who he meant, nor did I attempt lobbing anything as useless as a *she'll come around* at him. After fifteen years of not coming around, who was I to decree a change of heart?

I moved one chair closer.

"She tells Julie to tell me things, even when I'm in the room," he said, and then let out a bitter chuckle. "If she can even stand to be in the same room with me for that long."

He seemed in the mood for talking now, so I remained silent.

"Julie says it's because I look so much like Dad and it's hard for her to see so much of him in me now that he's gone. But, you know, I looked like Dad too when she threw me out, so I don't think that's the problem," he said, his voice quietly edging toward fury.

I rested a hand on his back, in the space between his shoulder blades. It was an inadequate gesture at best, but he didn't shove it off, so I left it there.

He sucked in a long, shuddery breath and gathered himself. "There's a reception in the other room," he said, suddenly realizing he was technically supposed to be in some kind of hosting capacity. "There's, I don't know, sandwiches and stuff."

"Do you want me to get you something?"

Nate shook his head.

"What do you want to do, Nate?" I asked softly.

He looked around the empty room, taking in its unfamiliar furnishings, the wallpaper that should have been stripped and redone a decade ago. His face crumpled in bewilderment, as though he couldn't figure out how he had even ended up here.

"I want to get out of here," he said, in the same tone of voice a much younger version of himself might have said *I want to go home.*

"Okay," I said. "Let's go."

I trundled him to my rental car, and for a moment we just sat there while whatever radio station I had half-listened to on the way here played a grating commercial for weight loss. Nate stared out the windshield, listening even less and providing no destination options.

Suspecting I would get none however long I waited, I keyed the ignition on and backed out of the parking space.

"Okay, I'm just going to drive. Stop me if you see something interesting, otherwise I will just keep going," I said. As an afterthought, I tacked on, "Keeping in mind that this car has no navigation system and I have never been in this town in my life. Or this state, for that matter."

He may have cracked a smile, but that might have just been wishful thinking on my peripheral vision's part.

We drove. I turned when I had to, or when the fancy tickled, more likely than not going in circles, though Nate didn't seem to mind.

"That's my high school," he said, pointing out the window to his right, when I found a new street to go down.

I slowed the car down to a crawl. It was late afternoon, so most of the kids were long gone, and the school building stood silent, a gray shell against a gray sky.

We circled the block, and Nate tapped his finger against the window as we passed the football field.

"And under that bleacher on the far end is where I got my first real kiss," he said, perking up a little at being able to share a memory from so long ago.

"Which is different from a first not-real kiss?" I said, squinting out the window, like if I squinted hard enough, I might just be able to make out the ghosts of a young Nate and his paramour in between the slats of the bleachers.

Nate smiled -- actually smiled this time; I saw it full on -- and said, with total assurance, "Dares and bottle-spinning don't count. It doesn't count if all you're feeling is complete embarrassment."

"This changes my life completely. All this time I thought Cindy Wells and I had something special in fifth grade," I said, earning a good-natured eye roll. "Who was the lucky guy -- your first real kiss?"

"That would be a fine young man by the name of Jason Sandoval. He was a year older. He was in the debate club, so kind of a nerd--"

"Hey, hey," I interrupted, "I did debate in high school. We were exceptionally cool."

"--but," Nate continued pointedly, steamrolling right over my interjection, "I really liked him."

I looked over at him as we left the school behind and came to a red light. "So, young Jason was in debate and therefore incredibly cool," I said, "and how about you? High school you?"

One side of his mouth tilted upward. "Less cool," he said, leaving it at that, his lips playing with a smile, remembering something that existed only in his head as far as he was concerned.

"That's all you're going to tell me? Less cool?" I shook my head, dissatisfied. "I'm going to ask Julie for yearbook pictures."

At the mention of her name, I felt Nate shift uncomfortably.

"Emory. Why are you here?" he asked.

"I told you; Julie called. She thought you might want a familiar face around," I said.

"I'm sorry she dragged you out here. She doesn't really get the concept of minding her own business sometimes."

I couldn't tell from his tone whether he was frustrated, whether he meant it in displeasure. I glanced at him quickly in between long views of the road but couldn't get a good read on him that way either; maybe driving around while having this conversation wasn't the safest idea in the world.

"Um, if you're mad," I said, trying simultaneously to be placating and to read a street sign, "don't be mad at her, okay? I mean, yes, she did call me and ask me to come, but it was my decision in the end, so if you're mad, please be mad at me."

Nate looked my way. "I'm not."

"Oh. Okay."

"Thank you for coming."

It wasn't the same as saying *I'm glad you're here*, but I didn't push it.

"Of course," I said.

There was a lot more I wanted to say than that, but it was also the kind of thing you had to actually sit down with someone and look them in the eye to be able to say it properly. Things like *Hey, we should get some ice cream* pass as acceptable conversational sallies in a moving vehicle; things like *I love you and I look like a zombie when you're gone, please come back to me so I can stop scaring the small children in my building* usually do not.

I stopped the car on the side of the road.

Nate looked at our surroundings, confused as to why I had pulled over in front of a derelict single-story with a dry-cleaning sign one thunderstorm away from falling off completely.

"Nate," I said. "I, uh..."

I couldn't finish. Not because I didn't mean it, not because I didn't want to say it, but because he looked at me then with such a lost, fragile air that I couldn't.

Of course I couldn't. What kind of insensitive lunatic tries to win his ex-boyfriend back when his ex-boyfriend's father has just died?

In my defense, I was running on a profound lack of sleep, plus the fumes of a broken relationship. But even so, I'd probably have cast my vote with the prosecution. I was being an insensitive lunatic, and this was neither the time nor the place for me to show him just how much sanity I did not possess.

"I'm here for you, okay? Whatever you need," I said. Nice save, Emory.

"Yeah," he said, dredging up a smile from some hidden reserve.

"Well," I said, peering out the window at the empty, peeling husk of someone's dry-cleaning dreams, "is there anything else in town you want to see?"

He looked around apologetically. "Uh, I don't actually know where we are right now."

"And that's why you should never let me drive you around indiscriminately," I said, sagaciousness very much becoming me.

"Oh, I see," Nate said, a smile behind his mildly affronted tone. "So you're saying this is my fault?"

"Yeah, the thing is," I said, taking on facetiousness as a second hobby, which incurred a raised eyebrow on Nate's part, "I did absolve myself of all responsibility before we set off, and since there are only two of us in the car, it stands to reason that this falls entirely on you, my friend."

"Man," Nate said, shaking his head with deepest disapproval, "if we ran out of gas you'd be the kind of person who would make me walk ten miles to the next station for gas, wouldn't you?"

I smiled serenely. "And a soda."

Nate laughed, though he then made a face as though he hadn't expected to hear that sound coming from himself. "You're the worst," he said softly.

"I know."

He looked down at his hands. "I'm glad you're here."

I had earned it after all.

"Me too," I said. "Although, obviously, not ideal circumstances. But it's good to see you. I mean, again, not ideal circumstances."

"Yeah, no, I know what you mean," he said, glancing at me out of the corner of his eye.

I restrained myself from reaching out to touch him, instead asking, "Well, think we should drive around like we know what we're doing for the next hour before finally asking someone for directions?"

"That absolutely sounds like something we would do," Nate approved.

"Okay, but just remember that this was your idea," I said, pulling back out onto the road.

Nate didn't say anything, but he was biting his thumbnail with a smile on his lips as he looked out the window to the trees and sky cruising past us.

As occasionally happens, an occurrence not rare enough to make our half of the species relinquish the idea that asking for directions is beneath us, Nate and I eventually started recognizing a handful of street names as we passed their signs.

Well, Nate did more than I, but he'd come with the advantage of having lived here before. I am just a quick learner.

Once we hit a pair of cross streets he definitely knew, it was smooth sailing from there, though the closer we got to wherever he was directing me, the lower he seemed to sag into the passenger seat.

I understood once we pulled into a residential cul de sac and he called the car to a stop at the end of the driveway of a colonial-style two-story home with pale yellow siding and a modest front yard. I could imagine him in his early childhood ruining the grass by triking all over it, as I had in my parents' yard way back when.

They hadn't been too pleased but then took a photo anyway of me reigning over my minute destruction.

"Have you been staying here?" I asked, looking out at the house. The roof still had a lone string of Christmas lights hanging from its eaves.

Lights were on inside; out where we were, what had been a slate gray kind of day deepened into charcoal.

"Julie insisted," Nate said. "She said it would be stupid for me to spend money on a hotel when I could just come home. I don't know how she talked our mother into it, especially when Mom can barely stand to look at me. I think she might just be tolerating my presence for Abby's sake."

His facial expression told me as much, but I remarked anyway, "Must be hard for you."

Nate took his time responding. "It hasn't changed a lot, inside," he said at length. "There are times when I can almost feel like things aren't the way they are."

I knew what he meant. It's those kinds of feelings that are often the most insidious, because when you do remember the way things truly are, it hits twice as hard. It wasn't difficult to imagine the struggle he'd had to undergo these past few days, walking through the corridors of a home that had turned him out long ago.

Before I could think to stop myself, I said, "You're welcome to stay with me if you want, at my hotel. I mean, there's two beds in there, so it wouldn't be-- It's not like-- Uh."

A corner of his mouth lifted slightly. "It's okay, calm down. I know you're not trying to seduce me. Or if you are, you're doing it really badly," Nate said, giving me a vaguely amused, dubious look.

"I don't know any other way," I said, shrugging.

"That is such a lie," he said placidly.

I wasn't sure where this line of conversation was headed, so I didn't say anything.

"I do want to come and stay with you," Nate said eventually and slowly, as though saying it aloud was the actual process of making up his mind. "If the offer's still on the table."

"It's permanently on the table," I said, getting very, very far ahead of myself and afield of the current situation. It was too much to take back, so I plowed on. "Do you have stuff you need to get from the house?"

"Yeah, and I should probably talk to Julie at least," he said, taking a brief moment for himself, and then got out of the car.

I watched him walk up the driveway and through the front door, and wondered how he could even do it without bending under the weight of all that strain.

Julie had probably had the right intentions in talking both parties into having Nate stay here, just as she had with getting me to come. It wasn't a totally unreasonable expectation -- tragedy often brought people closer together; the jolt of realization that life was insistently ephemeral made petty arguments seem negligible after all.

But, apparently, not always.

Nate emerged within about ten minutes with a duffel bag in hand, Julie walking with him back out to the car.

I got out, unlocking the trunk for Nate's things.

"Hi, Emory," Julie said as they approached. "I'm glad you could come."

"Yeah, absolutely. Thanks for getting in touch with me," I said.

Nate slung his bag into the trunk, and he and Julie shared a tight hug. When he got into the car and we waved goodbye, Julie told me to take care of him, and I had the inexplicable feeling that she was passing some kind of torch to me. She had looked out for Nate since they were kids, and now it was my turn.

It seemed a presumptuous move, to be honest, but also to be honest, it was a move I didn't mind at all. Where Nate actually stood on the matter was a different story and currently a closed book to me.

We were still broken, after all. Just because I had come and he hadn't made me leave didn't mean we were fixed.

The hotel was about a ten-minute drive away, and we made the journey in total silence. The radio tried to cheer us up with a string of peppy golden oldies, but it served only to highlight the depth of the gloom in the car.

It had been Nate's choice this time, his escape, but I didn't suppose leaving home again was much easier the second time around when nothing else had changed from the first.

I remembered the night in Thailand when I'd had my first of many inner crises and Nate simply giving me a hug with no expectations attached, and when we got inside the hotel room, I returned the favor. He seemed not to mind, leaning heavily into me, his face pressed into my shoulder.

There didn't seem anything else to do after that except crawl into bed -- separate beds -- and go to sleep with dreams of something better in the morning.

Sleep chose not to come, though, for either of us. I could hear him, across the aisle between our beds, shifting and twisting underneath the covers, while I stared up into the dark, wishing I could just reach over and soothe him to sleep.

"Emory," he said finally. It wasn't a whisper, so he obviously knew I was lying awake too.

"Yup."

More shuffling, probably to turn toward my bed. "This is weird," he said.

"What's weird?"

"That we're in the same room, but you're so far away."

"It's, like, two feet."

Nate was quiet for a moment. "You're being deliberately obtuse."

"Yes."

"Why?"

I sighed, a long exhalation. "It's not me, it's you."

The light on the nightstand between our beds snapped on, and there was Nate propped up on one elbow, looking in my direction with what would have probably been an affronted expression on his face, were it not for the substantial amount of squinting he was doing.

"That light is extremely bright," I said, shielding myself from its glare with one arm.

Nate tossed a pillow at me to get it down. "What do you mean it's not you?"

"It's not me," I reiterated, probably unhelpfully. "Under different circumstances I would have tried to-- to do many, many things by now."

He eyed me with sullen suspicion. "Like what?"

"Like say I'm sorry," I said, turning to face him at last, "for hiding what we had from everyone. And say I'm sorry for putting you through all my bullshit. I'm surprised you're still willing to even look at me after all that. And say I'm sorry in general for, um, umbrella coverage of any other stupid things I did."

Nate looked away for a moment, ruminating on my apology. "What else?" he demanded.

"Tell you that I told everyone," I said. "Although, to be perfectly honest, I haven't gotten around to my parents yet. But I was going to, when Julie called."

I could see that he was having an internal battle with himself, curious to know the details of what telling everyone meant but still wanting more of the list of my many, many things.

"What else?" he decided.

"Tell you that Michelle's gone, that if I had been more honest with myself she would've been gone a lot sooner," I admitted. I had the feeling he was going to what else me again, so I carried on, cresting on a wave of words kept for too long to myself. "Tell you that I miss you so much it hurts, and I can't sleep, and it's making me look like an extra in a horror movie."

We were both gathered at the edges of our beds now, knowing full well we could step over the two-foot divide at any time but fearful that traversing the connection would break it somehow.

Nate took a deep breath. Somehow knowing I had more, or hoping I had more, he said again, "What else?"

I glanced down at the carpet. "Kiss you."

"So kiss me."

"No."

"Or be really infuriating."

"That I can do," I said, as he glared at me. I softened my tone immeasurably. "Nate, you're hurting. Letting me seduce you, however ineptly, isn't going to make it go away."

The glare remained. "I'm a grown man, Emory. I'm capable of making rational decisions."

"That doesn't mean they won't be bad decisions."

Nate made a loud noise of aggravation. "Don't patronize me," he said, flinging the comforter off as though it had done him a grave wrong. He swung his legs out into the divide and crossed it, looming over me. "Move over, asshole."

"What? What are you doing? This is untoward," I protested, as he rolled me over to the far side of the bed and climbed in.

He settled himself neatly under the covers a chaste distance away from me, looking up at the ceiling, seemingly content now that he had finished making a nuisance of himself.

"Are you happy now?" I asked, punching his shoulder ineffectually.

Nate turned away from the ceiling to look at me. "You can't say all those things to me and expect me not to want to come over and say I miss you too."

An ember of hope glowed in my chest, but I ignored it, carrying on in the vein of being put-upon. "You know, you could've done that without forcibly displacing me."

"That was for saying all those things and not doing anything about it."

"I'm being noble, all right? Besides, it would be a really bad idea," I said. "I know you know it as well as I do."

Nate sighed, which was as good as getting verbal agreement. He reached over to the nightstand and shut the light off. Under the covers, our hands found each other; our fingers twined together, good enough for now, and sleep finally found us.

Chapter Thirteen

Morning was a different beast altogether.

I awoke with Nate lying half on top of me, the side of his face mashed into the pillow, sleeping the sleep of thorough exhaustion.

If things were different, if things were how they had been before, I would simply have put my arm around him to draw him nearer and fall back asleep, enveloped in him. How many mornings had I done it, how many times had I'd squandered the luxury of doing it unaware that there would be an end date in sight? Enough times to become a habit; too few to even come close to losing its thrill.

If things were different, I would wake him up with a kiss, or if I was feeling particularly suicidal, a jab to his side.

If things were different, I wouldn't be thinking about it, I'd just do it.

I ran the pad of my thumb over his jawline, fitting the curve of my palm over it, molded seamlessly together, like that was where it belonged from the beginning.

Funny how you can still have the muscle memory for something even after a long absence; of course, it's all a matter of the strength of neuronal connections in the brain and body, but I preferred to think that I was just meant for waking up every morning next to Nate and knowing exactly what to do.

Except, of course, that I didn't know what the hell I was doing.

Carefully, I extricated myself from Nate; he was too far gone to even notice, his limbs leaden with sleep.

When I finished showering and got dressed, I emerged from the bathroom to find Nate sitting up in bed, blinking, his hair a mess, creases in his face where he'd been sleeping on the pillow.

"Hey," I said, leaning against the wall.

"Hi," Nate said blearily.

He rubbed his face, reddening his stubbled cheeks. When his eyes cleared it looked as though it had come back to him why he was here in the first place, in this hotel room, with me on the opposite side of it. A deep sigh rattled out of his throat.

"Do you ever wish," he asked, "that you could be somebody different?"

"Most days," I said, coming over to sit on the other bed. "Who do you want to be?"

Nate shrugged, picking at a corner of the comforter nestled over his legs. "Somebody whose last words to his dad could've been three days ago, instead of fifteen years."

The saddest thing was that he so clearly still loved them, was so clearly still hoping to be forgiven for something he had as much control over as he did the direction of the earth's rotation. Or maybe the saddest thing was that he was hoping for forgiveness, when he should be the one asked to grant it.

"Don't do that to yourself," I said. "None of it is your fault."

"I just--" He shook his head, unable to finish the thought. "Who would you be?"

"Somebody more like you."

Nate frowned, nonplussed. "Have you seen me recently? I'm a mess."

"Being sad doesn't make you a mess."

"Pretty sure I look it, though," he said, running a hand through his hair, which didn't help to tame it any.

"Yeah," I said flatly. "It's pretty rough. Soon you'll only be able to book modeling jobs for department store circulars in the Sunday papers."

His shoulders shook with a short laugh. "The horror."

Feeling slightly less of a mess for the moment, Nate slid out of bed and headed for the bathroom, while I, having nothing better to do, retrieved my laptop and meandered about the Internet, looking for things to do. The burial wasn't until tomorrow, and today was the space in between.

I didn't know what Nate was going to do; it seemed like there must be something, there was always something else, something more to do when someone died, making sure each detail would meet the approval of someone who wouldn't even see.

Nate didn't know either.

"My mother won't let me help with anything. It's probably more work for her to have to tell Julie to tell me what to do," he said.

So we drove out to the coast, less than an hour away. In the summer it probably did a roaring business, but we were still on the cusp seasonally, winter still clinging on by its fingernails while spring tried to pry them off one by one, and there was no business to be had.

Outside of us, there was a single beachcomber with a metal detector and hopes of buried jetsam ambling along the shore, just out of reach of the waves as they rushed in to play tag with him.

We sat on a bench, swaddled in hooded sweatshirts, and watched the progress of his fruitless scavenge, thick clouds above turning everything into a muted gray version of itself.

Once the man passed out of our sights, following the shoreline into eternity as far as we knew, Nate turned to me. "Yesterday, when you said you told everyone, what did you mean?"

"Everyone important, I guess. I mean, aside from my parents," I said. "I didn't rush out to inform my mailman or anything."

"Oh, he knows," Nate said offhandedly.

"Oh. Okay," I said, thrown. "Well, I guess I can cross him off the list. But people at work know. I suspect it was the hot topic of conversation yesterday and will continue to be for some time whenever I'm out of earshot."

"Why?"

"Uh, because the last interesting thing that happened was someone breaking her leg six months after she broke her arm while skiing, and she's all better now, so unfortunately it's going to be me for a while, until something more exciting comes along," I explained. "Fingers crossed for the other ulna to get fractured within the week."

Nate looked at me, dissatisfied with my treatise on the vagaries of water-cooler talk. "I meant, why tell anyone?"

"Because I realized you were right about pretty much everything," I said.

He grinned. "Well, I very much like the sound of that."

"I assume it's the novelty of it that you find so exhilarating, since it gets said to you so infrequently? Ow," I laughed, jerking away from the vicious prod his fingers delivered to my waist.

"You're an ass," he said, undercutting it with a smile toward the sky.

"Yeah, well," I said to his upturned profile, "you're the one who still likes me, so."

His smile widened. "Is this how you plan to win every argument we ever have?"

"I don't know," I said, studying him carefully. "Were you planning to have a lot of arguments with me in the future?"

Nate turned his gaze to mine and held it steady. "Can we?"

The bank of embers in my chest sparked up to full flame, immolating my uncertainties to ash and brightening my face with a wide grin. "Yes," I said simply.

He tried to bite down a smile. "Good."

"In that case, I'll have to mix it up so we don't get stale," I said. "So once in a while I'll resort to name-calling, too, and maybe pull your hair."

"That sounds amazing," Nate said, laughing. "I can't wait for our next fight."

"Why wait?" I said recklessly, unable to tamp down my happiness -- and frankly, after everything, why should I? "Your gloves are stupid, and I can't believe you wasted good American dollars on not one but two pairs of those things. There, I said it."

Nate looked at me, tickled. "Not this again. You're never going to let this go, are you?"

"I don't know, you think you can make me?" I goaded, tipping exceedingly into his personal space.

He leaned into mine. "I know I can," he said, in that honey-dipped voice I knew so well. "My sources tell me I can be extremely persuasive."

As we ditched the argument in favor of skipping right to making up, it was hard to say who closed the distance first, not that it mattered in the greater scheme of things. I couldn't remember when I'd had a more satisfying fake fight.

My fingers dug furrows into his hair, and his gripped at my back, clutching me closer and closer as if the laws of physics would even allow it. There were tongues and teeth, and gasped, airless breaths, searing brands onto each other's skin, the heat between us blindingly delicious as a dying winter wind coiled around us, as though hoping to preserve us forever in that moment.

With great effort, Nate wrenched himself backwards. "Wait, wait," he said. "We can't do this here."

I blinked at him stupidly, the haze of lust yet to lift. As I looked around I realized he had a point. There was no one around, but we were smack in the middle of an open beach, and it probably wouldn't be an auspicious start to our re-acquaintance if we both got charged with public indecency.

Nate shoved his fingers into my sweatshirt pocket, pulling out the car keys, which he then dumped into my hand. "Drive," he said.

We raced each other back to the car, wild with purpose, and couldn't help but kiss fiercely again once we got inside.

"Okay, okay," I said finally, sticking, with slight difficulty, the key into the ignition. "Driving now. No touching rule in effect immediately."

"This is going to be the longest hour of my life," Nate complained, making a point to sit on his hands as I peeled out of the parking lot and out onto the main road, back toward the highway.

"Hey," I said, taking higher ground, "you're the one who suggested we drive all the way out here. You have only yourself to blame."

He laughed. "There's nothing else to do out here. Besides, if you hadn't been so intent on being noble yesterday, we could have been having sex at least twelve hours ago."

"Twelve hours ago, we hadn't gotten back together," I pointed out.

"Twelve hours ago, I loved you just as much as I do now," he countered.

I very slowly applied the brakes, rolling the car to a stop along an empty parking lane, and put it in park, plus the emergency handbrake. "Did you just...?"

"Yes," said Nate, straightforward and unflinching.

I bit the inside of my lip. "Well, twelve hours ago, so did I."

He beamed at me. "That is such a sneaky way of getting out of saying it."

"Nate," I said. "I love you."

"That's better," he said, and took the opportunity, now that our vehicle was stationary, to unclick both our seatbelts and pull me into a long kiss.

Now that our respective cats were out of their bags, off somewhere making best friends with each other, it felt as though there was a different quality to our kiss now, charged but languid, intense but indulgent, like we had all of forever to sort them out. And maybe we did.

"Okay," Nate said at length, "I really want to take this fucking sweatshirt off you, so we should probably start driving again before I haul you off to the backseat."

I agreed, releasing the handbrake, and drove as fast as I dared.

The minute our hotel room door eased shut, my back hit the wall, Nate pressing me up against it, his mouth on mine, his hands diving underneath my sweatshirt, burning their imprints into my skin.

I never wanted to stop touching him or for him to stop touching me; even the mere seconds away necessary to shuck our clothing seemed beyond excessive.

Finally getting them out of the way, we staggered, entangled and lost in each other, toward the nearest bed, falling in a heap as soon as the back of my knees hit its edge. His hands glided along my sides with a sweet smoothness as we slid up the bed, freshly made and chocolate-minted.

There were a million things lighting my senses on fire all at once, his day-old stubble grazing my chin, his fingertips tattooing their pinpoints into my back, the salt on the skin at his neck, the sound that emerged from his throat when I licked into its hollow.

I burned underneath his touch, underneath his tongue, a trail of dirty, incendiary kisses everywhere he could reach.

The million things coalesced into one bright spark as Nate pushed me over the edge and sent my senses soaring wild, tethered only by his body, by his lips murmuring into my skin how to find my way back.

Chapter Fourteen

The morning of the burial, I wasn't quite sure what to expect. We hadn't talked about it the day prior, focusing on and reveling only in having wound our ways back to each other, exploring our relationship in its newness all over again.

Nate dressed slowly, taking his time with the cuffs on his shirt, the buttons of his jacket. He looked at himself in the mirror for a long time after he was done, but I didn't think he was really seeing himself there.

Just to feel useful, I straightened his tie, and he smiled. It came easily to him.

"I'm glad you're here," he said again, as I dusted specks of nothing off his shoulders.

"I'm here," I said. Where else could I be?

We drove to the church under a light drizzle, such a trite convention that it seemed as though somebody had ordered it off a funeral checklist.

The rest of Nate's family was already gathered in the front pew when we arrived. I folded my hand over his briefly, imparting in silence whatever courage or conviction he might need in addition to his abundance, and hung back as he made his way to join them in front of the apse of the church.

Like I had at the memorial service, I stayed toward the back of the church, keeping Nate in my sights. I kept watch still when the sermon had been said and the eulogy over, when the coffin was picked up and carried out the back of the church by people I didn't know. Nate hadn't been asked to be one of the pallbearers.

After the casket was transferred to the hearse, Nate opted not to ride with his family to the cemetery, coming to find me in the parking lot instead.

At the other end of the lot, Julie waved. Picking up on it, Abby spotted me and followed suit, turning to her mother as she did so, probably to ask why her old speech therapist was in attendance.

It is a little known fact of our distinguished profession that we all enjoy cultivating friendly relations with all of our clients' uncles. It's just one of the many services we provide.

I returned the gesture to both of them and unlocked the car. "Your mother is looking suspiciously this way," I said, wondering if I should wave at her too to be polite.

I did, even though she had no idea who I was, other than as a person standing next to her son, and it was probably the rules of newspaper column etiquette that made her acknowledge me with a curt nod.

"Well, you know, she's probably judging you as we speak," Nate said, casting a quick eye toward her as she folded herself into Julie's car, "and going through a laundry list of egregious sins you're likely to have committed."

"Oh, yeah, I do tons of those," I said. "Keeps my brain sharp."

"Yeah, I can think of a few you're really good at," Nate said with a wry smile.

"Well, if she's judging me as I am now, at least I look nice, right?" I said, glancing down at my suit. "I mean, the guy who sold me this was thoroughly adamant that it did."

He chuckled softly. "You're just fishing for compliments now."

We got into the car and followed the line of the others behind the hearse, heading toward the cemetery. When we reached, I once again left Nate unaccompanied to take his place with his family at the side of the grave.

Maybe one day we would walk toward them together, hand in hand, but today was not that day, and now was not the time.

Instead, I joined the small, remaining throng of guests in the informal semi-circle they had made around the burial plot. The same drizzle was still misting over the grounds, bowing everybody's heads.

The coffin lowered into its final resting place.

Nate hesitated, and then put a hand on his mother's shoulder, squeezing it gently. She froze, stuck in a long moment of indecision, and finally lifted her hand and placed it over his, and she squeezed back.

It was all she gave him, and it wasn't much, but I suppose it was a start.

As the guests began to disperse, I walked back to the car to wait for Nate.

"I saw that, with your mom," I said, when he appeared at last. "That was good."

He shrugged and ran a quick hand under his nose. "It's something."

"Come here," I said, wrapping my arms around him, keeping him warm until the drizzle stopped.

"Hey," he said. "Let's go home."

***

It took another week for life to settle back down to manageable proportions.

People at work eyed me with varying degrees of suspicion or approbation, and a couple of them mistook me for the kind of guy who knew twelve different ways to tie a scarf and whether that scarf clashed with their purse. My helpful tip that most accessories were just needless expenses met with disappointment.

At home, my bathroom sink went back to its glory days of accommodating two toothbrushes on its stone countertop, plus a whole host of hair products it took a better man than me to understand.

And that man sat with me and held my hand when I picked up the phone to finally call my parents.

The answering machine picked up, cheery. "Hi, you've reached the Jameses. We're not home, so leave a message. Have a great day!"

"Hey, Mom and Dad. It's, um-- It's me," I said. "Obviously. Unless you know somebody else who calls you Mom and Dad. Uh, anyway. I wanted to see if you guys were going to be around this weekend so I can come by for a bit. There's something really important that I want to talk to you about."

I paused and took a deep breath. Nate squeezed my hand.

"Okay. Call me."

About the Author

Cary Attwell lives in Seattle, Washington, where it rains and rains like the dickens, except when it doesn't. Fretting occurs on a daily basis, and small acts of idiocy are perpetrated with stunning proficiency much more often.

Ramble to or get rambled at about all kinds of nothing at the following:

Email: caryattwell@gmail.com

Twitter: http://www.twitter.com/caryattwell

Livejournal: http://www.caryattwell.livejournal.com

Goodreads: http://www.goodreads.com/caryattwell

Acknowledgements

Massive thank yous are in order:

To my disgustingly brilliant sister J, who went through every single draft of this book with me with patience, good humor and an eagle eye to put all eagles to shame, and kept challenging me to make it better.

To Mel, for reading the final draft over before I sicced it on everyone else and leaving me comments in the margins that made me laugh and laugh. (Go you!)

To Jen, who let me talk at her at length about the minutiae of the book for weeks on end over hotpot and board games, and inexplicably still seems to want to be friends with me.

To Julie Bozza, wonderful writer and all-around lovely human being, for talking me through the self-publishing process when I had no idea what I was doing.

To everyone who's ever encouraged me to write, for getting me here.

To my parents, for everything.

Printed in Great Britain
by Amazon.co.uk, Ltd.,
Marston Gate.